Haunted

Haunted

LYNN CARTHAGE

KENSINGTON BOOKS
www.kensingtonbooks.com

KENSINGTON BOOKS are published by

Kensington Publishing Corp.
119 West 40th Street
New York, NY 10018

All Kensington titles, imprints, and distributed lines are available at special quantity discounts for bulk purchases for sales promotions, premiums, fund-raising, educational, or institutional use.

Special book excerpts or customized printings can also be created to fit specific needs. For details, write or phone the office of the Kensington special sales manager: Kensington Publishing Corp., 119 West 40th Street, New York, NY 10018, attn: Special Sales Department; phone: 1-800-221-2647.

ISBN-13: 978-1-61773-626-1
ISBN-10: 1-61773-626-0

First Trade Paperback Printing: March 2015

10 9 8 7 6 5 4 3 2 1

Printed in the United States of America

First electronic edition: March 2015

ISBN-13: 978-1-61773-629-2
ISBN-10: 1-61773-629-5

Haunted

CHAPTER ONE

Offered for immediate sale: outstanding 18th-century stone manor built in 1721 for French expatriate family. In failing condition, the house is nonetheless a must-see for history lovers. Three grand stories sit on 30,000 acres, with plenty of room for development. Offered at a bargain by American heir overseas. Please enquire at Hamilton & Sons Estate Agents, 9 Princes Square, Grenshire.

—*Grenshire Argus* advertisement, run
September 30, 2009–present

*Y*ou know you've done something pretty awful when your family moves because of it. Not just within San Francisco, nor within California . . . not even within the country.

My stepdad, Steven, has a remote job, so it was no problem for him to relocate. Mom is a stay-at-home mom for Tabby; her job "traveled," too. As for me, they unenrolled me from school just a month before sophomore year ended.

Crazy.

When you're a major screwup, it helps if your stepdad has an ancestral mansion in England ready to move into. Well, not exactly *ready*. It's been uninhabited for a long time and needs some serious TLC, I heard him tell Mom.

He'd been trying to sell it for years. But at least it's a place to live, and a place for me to reflect on my behavior and improve it.

My therapy would be a lot more effective if I could remember what I did.

Emerging from the tunnel of trees to the clearing where we could finally see my stepfather's manor, I let out a moan of disillusionment. This wasn't the crumbling but still-impressive castle surrounded by broad, grassy lawns I'd imagined back in California, with swans wafting snootily around a lily-ponded lake. Instead, it was a grim, stone-walled prison with the grounds so overgrown they were nearly impenetrable.

I had allowed myself to become interested, had thought there was a lovely poetry to the phrase, "ancestral mansion in England." But nothing could quell the immediate sense of grinding apprehension the manor gave me. Nothing about it felt right.

As we drove up into its shadow, the manor leaned down over us to look. More than idly curious, it practically rubbed its leathern hands together in glee. *Visitors. At last.*

It was built in the shape of a U, making it hard to see where exactly one of the wings ended since it was lost somewhere to our left in a thick group of trees. The central courtyard that we inched along was cobblestoned, the size of a grand but cheerless park.

"Um, how many ancestors did you *have?*" I asked.

"It does seem large for one family," Steven answered, sighing and looking at Mom. "The Arnauds were very powerful and wealthy in the early 1700s when this was built."

"And the size of our family . . ." said Mom. Steven reached over and touched her cheek.

"We'll make it work," he said. He parked the car, turned off the engine, and got out. Mom sat there for a while, then turned around to check on Tabitha, my little sister, still sleeping in her car seat.

I got out and looked up at the Arnaud house while Steven started pulling luggage out of a hard plastic carrier atop the car. When I looked all the way to the top of the manor, my neck strained with the effort, my head hanging back heavily. *God, how big is this place?* There were hundreds of windows, dozens of gables, and a million stone designs of birds and beasts carved into the dark stone walls.

The manor's heavy breath stirred the hairs on the back of my neck. It surveyed me. It examined Mom and Steven and Tabby. Each of the windows looked smeared with time, but it seemed like the house could still see through them.

It would be easy to get lost in a house that size—and no one would find you.

I turned around and looked at the surrounding forest, ragged with illicit shrubs. It didn't look like any gardeners came to take care of this overwrought mess.

"No neighbors?" Mom asked.

Steven shook his head. "I think the original landhold-ings were even larger. There's no one else around for miles. This is the only house on Auldkirk Lane."

Mom unbuckled Tabby and pulled her out. "Welcome to your new home, sweetie," she said. My little sister rubbed her gray eyes, which were huge in her tiny face. She was wearing a headband with a pink flower on it, crooked from her nap. When she turned her head to look at the manor, I could see a tuft of snarled auburn hair in the back.

Steven grabbed the biggest suitcase, my mom's. I ex-pected him to head toward the double wooden doors that clearly marked the main entry, but he ducked into a smaller door on the right wing, marked with a small stone roof.

"You'll be relieved," he called over his shoulder, "to see our quarters aren't quite as ancient as the rest of the house. The information the real estate people sent me was that there is a very comfortable living space in the east wing."

Mom and Tabby went inside directly behind him, and I heard Mom coo in amazement. I hesitated outside, un-willing to go through the portal and enter the house's in-fluence. I waited, listening to the wind sing through the tree canopy. This was our new home. Because of me.

I lowered my head and followed them in—and saw why Mom was so surprised.

It was completely modern inside. Well, modern as of the 1970s. The living room had plaid and leather sofas, adorned with small circular pillows. The rug was a shag sunrise, as the colors moved in a rippling line from pale yellow to bright gold. Giant orbs hung on linked chains from the ceiling, hovering over the furniture to provide lighting.

Mom and I walked into the kitchen, which had avocado-colored appliances. With a little smile, she tried out the stove's gas burners. "Well, at least I won't have to use a cauldron," she murmured.

Behind the kitchen was a den, with a pigeonholed desk, a leather armchair, and a standing floor lamp whose lampshade was decorated with orange and brown stripes.

I looked for the bedrooms next. Oddly, there was a nursery with a crib and a dresser with waddling ducks painted on each drawer. I had to think: Had Steven said he'd been born in this house? Maybe this had been his room once.

The master bedroom, oversized and smelling slightly stuffy, was clearly not for me.

My room had a twin bed covered in a bright green spread, with matching carpet. If the room had windows, I was sure the drapes would have been the same glaring green. The effect was that I was a worm who'd burrowed into the dark heart of a lime.

On the plus side, the room was as large as a master suite, and the tiny bed viewed from the door looked like a forgotten slipper in a queen's dressing room. My room in California had been pretty small; this had possibility. I could have a lot of friends over. That is, if I could make some here in Grenshire.

I didn't mind leaving behind my stuff; everything was

from IKEA anyway. Maybe Mom and I could cruise yard sales and do a shabby chic thing for my room.

A mirror hung above the dresser. I didn't look that bad, considering everything I'd been through. My long auburn hair was still reasonably wavy and I didn't need concealer to hide circles under my green eyes.

I'm not a knockout but last year I did manage to snag one of the hottest guys in school, Richard Spees. Total surprise here, because guys don't stop in the school hallway and pivot to keep their eyes on girls like me. I've seen that happen a lot, but always to someone else.

Luckily, I'm an athlete—a swimmer—so at least I don't worry about my weight, although I would really, really like to get rid of that one huge mole right in my cleavage. What little there is of that, that is. I definitely fail the pencil test Bethany told me about—it's when you put a pencil horizontally under your boob and see if it stays by itself.

I read constantly, and subsequently have the kind of vocabulary that makes English teachers' eyes light up (which doesn't exactly help with the guys, but I can't prevent the stuff that comes out of my mouth). Last year I took a creative writing class, and found something I thought I could be good at. I could be a swimming author. A literary mermaid.

I sat down on the edge of the bed. I didn't mind the color scheme, but the room had hardly any light. Why no windows? It sucked not to be able to get some fresh air. Maybe whoever designed this was worried about teens sneaking out the window at night.

I returned to the living room with a big sigh. "My room's acid green," I announced. No one said anything, and I gritted my teeth. They would see it as a complaint, and here I was trying to be a better daughter. Mom and Steven's parenting technique: ignores anything verging on whining. "It's okay," I amended. "Green's good."

Still no response.

"I'm sorry," I said.

Steven rescued me. "Any interest in seeing the rest of the house?" he asked, holding up what looked like floor plans.

"Yeah," I said. I gave him a big smile, but he wasn't ready to return it. Parents are so big on that punishment thing.

"Not right now," said Mom. "You go along. I'll stay with Tabby."

"You sure?" he asked.

"Yes," she said. "My guess is, it's not the safest place for babies. You scout it out first."

"I don't imagine it's babyproofed," he said drily, and she laughed.

"Tell me if you see those medieval outlet covers," she said.

"Medieval? It's not that old," he protested.

"Could've fooled me," she said with a grin.

"All right," he said. "If I'm not back in an hour, call the fire department because I've probably fallen through a rotten floorboard."

"That's all I need," she said. "Seriously, be safe."

He kissed her and Tabby, and went back outside, with

me following behind. The air was a little cooler now that it was late afternoon. I straightened my back; was someone watching me? It didn't help that the light was fading prematurely thanks to the intense foliage. The shadows of leaves agitated by the wind made strange patterns on the ground.

"Twilight at the haunted mansion," Steven intoned in a deep voice, and then he chuckled.

"Not so funny," I said. "There's a legitimate creep factor here."

He led me toward those big main doors I had seen before, and pulled from his pocket an enormous, antique-looking key. A man's anguished face made of iron was the lock; the key went into his open mouth. He looked like he was in the midst of a scream, and the key was meant to be his gag.

The doors were heavy. Steven's face turned red as he pushed one of them inward. It groaned like it hadn't been opened in centuries.

"Are you sure we should go in?" I asked.

"It'll be good to get some fresh air circulating," he said quietly.

Inside, *holy crap*. Huge. Dynastically huge. The entry hall with its vaulted ceiling was so large I could have thrown a rock with all my strength and it would only get halfway across the floor. The stones forming the floor were arranged in patterns of dark gray and lighter gray, creating a somber chessboard stretching into the distance.

The grand staircase at the other end was wide enough to hold dozens of people on each riser, and the chandelier hovering over us was so full of glass and iron that if it fell it would plow through the bedrock beneath the flooring, like a meteor. Most of one wall was taken up by a fireplace large enough to roast several standing horses— you know, if you ever wanted to.

The air felt museumlike. Cold. I tried to imagine the hall filled with life, lots of people in high ruffled collars smiling and laughing, and the sound of carriages rolling up to the entry outside, but all I could think was that all of them were long dead, and their dresses and breeches had rotted into sticky threads.

"Hello!" shouted Steven to the ceiling. It echoed back at him seconds later.

I wished he hadn't done that. It seemed—I don't know—just wrong somehow. He started toward the stairs, and when he was halfway there, I ran to catch up with him. The run was long enough that I was out of breath when I got there—and I'm the girl who can hold her breath. My lungs are hard as canteens from all my years of swimming.

I practically needed my passport to cross that room. The leaded glass windows, at varying levels in the walls, let in a filtered sunlight that made the place more disturbing. Gigantic cobwebs, or maybe they were spiderwebs, hung everywhere, stretched between light sconces like an ethereal tapestry.

The stairs were steep but seemed to draw me upward. *Come in, come in.*

I remembered my initial aversion to entering the manor . . . and now I was climbing up into its timeworn center. Some sort of invitation was being issued to me. Something lonely was made glad by our visit.

Steven climbed ahead of me; I kept some distance between us in case he started to fall. I didn't want to be a pair of dominoes with him.

Halfway up, I turned and looked down. Vertigo overcame me as I wavered there on the steps. For a second I was so sure I was going to fall that I clutched for the banister, furred with grime. After I steadied myself, I rubbed my hands on my jeans.

At the top of the stairs, I took a good look at the stained glass window that presided over the landing. Etched at the bottom was xxx, which made me snort because the image depicted was hardly X-rated. It showed two medieval knights. One was thrusting a spear into the other, who was rearing up with his sword. It looked like the one being impaled was going to seriously damage the other one when the sword came down.

Steven turned left, where he opened another set of double doors. We entered what had once been a ballroom. The curtains covering the floor-to-ceiling windows hung in shreds, their fibers simply too old to keep their shape against the sun's endless onslaught. The floor was a black-and-white marble parquet.

A trickle of sweat rolled from my temple. I felt like we were trespassing and were about to get caught at any minute. I wished Steven would walk a little more softly, but his heavy oxford shoes created their own small echo.

At the other end of the long room was an organ, large

as a church's. It dominated the space, looking like a miniature factory with all its pipes and bellows.

Steven took off his sweatshirt and used it to sweep dust off the organ bench. A cloud enveloped him and he began sneezing. "This better be worth it," he said. "I actually really like this shirt." His voice sounded brittle in the huge space.

He sat down and began pushing his feet alternately on two large, slanted wooden panels on the floor. I could hear a sort of wheeze or breath deep within the organ as it came to life. He pressed down one of the keys. Nothing happened, but as he continued to work the pedals, he pressed again and a slender noise came. As he pumped life into the mechanism, music emerged, his fingers moving swiftly over the keys, jumping from octave to octave. He performed something I recognized from the classical music station he always played in the car.

He pulled a round lever that said vox humana and the sound instantly changed, became eerily like monks singing in the distance, their voices drifting up from the monastery walls.

"I didn't know you could play," I said. He was a master, and I'd never seen him so much as look at a piano before, other than Tabby's four-key toy in the shape of a blue hippopotamus.

"God, it's been a long time," he said. He pressed another pedal and the sound became louder.

"You'll wake the dead," I said. I leaned over his right shoulder and tried to play my own chord. To his credit, he didn't try to rearrange my fingers like my old piano teacher used to. But he had already stopped working the pedals, so I didn't get to hear how monstrous and discordant my guess was.

The profound silence of the vast house settled around us. I had the strange feeling that the house or maybe the organ had not appreciated his sudden, forceful playing . . . as if he hadn't been respectful.

Please, get real, I told myself. *The house isn't angry at us.*

Steven stood up and the organ bench gave a stilted screech at the redistribution of weight. He tied his filthy sweatshirt around his waist and led me through an arched wooden door set in the side wall.

This next room was probably as big as the ballroom, but divided into three levels of bookshelves, ascending all the way up to the ceiling. The number of books was overpowering, and so was their odor. They were moldering, page by page, moisture making its way from the prefaces all the way through to the epilogues. Railings fenced in the three levels, making them resemble Spanish balconies. Narrow, rickety staircases—almost more like ladders—led up to each floor.

I climbed one of the staircases to see what kind of books rich people read in the 1700s. At the top level, I looked down at Steven, noticing the bald spot that his height normally hid, at least from me. He was reading the titles on one of the shelves, so I did the same, turning randomly to stare at the spines. Surprise: they were in French. But as I walked carefully across the balcony I saw some English titles, too, like *The Governance of Servants* and *Quelling Insubordination*.

After I came down, we walked room to room in silence, as if a deaf-mute real estate agent led us. The glut of rooms was dizzying: some chambers elevated by a few steps, other sunken. The house was a beehive with these dark interlocking cells. I imagined a gigantic queen bee, mistress of the hive, loping ahead of us, dragging her useless wings, to not be seen.

Once, after consulting his map, Steven knelt at a paneled wall and exposed what looked to be a cupboard but was actually the beginning of a passageway. After staring into its black depths for a moment, he closed it and said, "No, thanks." I laughed in agreement. Too claustrophobic.

At times, he jogged forward; at times, I had to stop and wait for him. I kept imagining hearing the swish of those giant bee wings, or maybe more like the sound of skirts, the way a small train would drag along the floor.

Somehow we emerged back in the great hall. It took me a second to recognize it from the different perspective.

"And that was just one wing of the house," said Steven. "Holy Christ."

I raised my eyebrows. Steven didn't usually swear in front of me. "You want to do the rest?" I asked. "I'm not tired."

He matter-of-factly folded his floor plans up and tucked them under his arm. "We'll save the rest for a rainy day," he said.

* * *

We went back to the apartment, where Mom and Tabby were playing with spoons on the living room floor. They hadn't been able to bring many of her toys, so apparently the flatware drawer was the new Babies R Us.

Now that I knew some of what lay beyond the zany brightness of these 1970s walls, I found it wasn't as easy to relax as before. Decay breathed behind the macramé. *That's pretty good,* I thought. *"Decay breathed behind the macramé." I could use that in a story.*

"What's it like?" asked Mom. Steven sat down on the floor next to her while I crashed on the sofa. For Tabby's amusement, he began drawing lines in the shag's pile with a soup spoon.

"Huge. Beautiful in a really decrepit way."

"So it won't be easy to make a showplace out of it."

He snorted. "It would be the project of the century."

"Sounds like just what we need," she said.

He snorted again.

"No, honestly," she said. "I need something to focus on. Anything we could sell to fund a renovation?"

"There's quite the library," said Steven. "I should get a rare books expert in here to inventory it."

"How come your mom didn't?" she asked.

"A commonsense thing like that would never have oc-curred to her. And she was never here long enough to put something like that into action." I saw the muscle at his jaw clench, just for a second.

He didn't like to talk about his mom. I had never met her.

"How long did she live here?" I asked.

"She and my father lived here less than a year, I think. She got pregnant with me, and he was abusive, so she fled back to the States to protect both of us."

My jaw dropped. I had never heard this. And from the look on Mom's face, neither had she. Steven was secretive about his family.

"He died soon afterward, so he was a nonevent as far as I'm concerned," Steven added.

"I'm really sorry," I said lamely. I didn't know what else to say. I was lucky that although my parents had separated, it wasn't until I was ten. And pretty much immediately Steven was on the scene, so I never went dadless.

"For anyone who would lift a hand to a child," said Steven, "death is a good answer."

"You mean . . . he hit her when she was pregnant?" Mom asked.

"That's what she told me."

That was a weird way to answer, especially with the tone of voice he used. He stared down at the runes his spoon had made. "Well, anyway, ancient history. It makes me think about the life I might've had if he was a different person. That nursery was meant for me, you know; I would have been raised as an Arnaud heir on the palatial grounds of his forebears."

"Would you have wanted to?" she asked dubiously.

"Well, things were much more in order back then," he

said. "The estate has been neglected for as long as I've been alive."

Personally, I didn't think the manor's crumbling was just from the last half century . . . things had been declining here for *way* longer than that.

"It's sad not to know your father," said Steven. "And that's the last I'm going to say on that."

Mom nodded wistfully, glancing over at me on the sofa. This was as much info on his family as we'd ever gotten. Mom had once warned me not to ask. It didn't make sense to press for more. He'd talk when he wanted to.

That night, I went to my lime-colored room. On a whim, I opened the dresser drawers to see neatly folded piles of my clothing. I hadn't had time to unpack, but Mom, God bless her, had done it for me. She must've filled the drawers while Steven and I were exploring the house. A little unnerved, I searched for my diary until I found it, still safely locked with the key in the toe of my candy-cane Christmas socks.

I sat down on my bed and let my mind drift back into a memory: Richard Spees stopping by our table in the cafeteria.

He's a senior and hot beyond belief. He stands right beside me, and I'm immediately thinking, *No way! He's standing by me?* Uma freezes, her french fry, coated with ketchup, halfway to her mouth. I straighten my posture and tuck my hair behind my ears.

"Hey, Phoebe, you looked good yesterday," he says.

"You were there?"

"I was."

"Thanks," I say, wishing I could come up with something cooler. Yesterday had been the swim meet against Oakland High. I'd torched them in the 100-meter freestyle, touching the wall what seemed like hours before anyone else. I think about how I must have looked from his eyes as I launched myself out of the pool in my school-colors-red-and-gold Speedo (last year, a few of us had petitioned for sexier, yet still aerodynamic, suits) and took all the high fives and wet hugs from my teammates. Finding out he had been looking at me when I didn't even know it makes me feel self-conscious.

"You looked good," he repeats, and suddenly I see it as a compliment to my body, rather than a sports-based comment on my performance.

I'm not going to say I completely take it in stride, because that doesn't happen. My cheeks burn with a really big blush, but I do manage to give a huge and hopefully sassy grin. Luckily, Bethany rescues me.

"Do you usually go to the swim meets?" she asks.

I throw her a grateful look, but before he can answer, she adds, "Or was there someone there you wanted to see?" I try to kick her under the table but get only her chair leg. She jolts backward a half inch in her plastic seat and laughs.

As I wait mortified for his response, it happens.

Stars swim up from behind my eyes, lazy and spectacular, taking the place of Bethany's gleeful face. The stars convey lightning bolts, too, and I'm dazzled and trying not to get hit. It's a slow lightning storm across the landscape of my vision, and as air creeps into my lungs, I submit.

Bethany tells me later that Richard said meaningfully, "There *was* someone I wanted to see," but all hell broke loose and people were yelling.

I wake up a few minutes after I passed out, Bethany says. Dozens of people cluster around me, and I'm lying facedown on the table. Ketchup from Uma's fries coats my hair. I raise my head, and the cafeteria aide helps me walk to the nurse's office.

I had fainted. Pretty dramatically.

It didn't cost me Richard Spees, even though I'd drooled while I was unconscious. "It didn't look great," admitted Bethany when I'd pressed her. Plus, there had been that ketchup masquerading as hair gel. Yet Richard had risen above all his gentlemanly disgust and somehow considered me attractive, even while lifting me from the table like a beached jellyfish and slapping me.

We dated for three excruciating months. He turned out to be a darb (dramatically asinine random boy) who prattled on and on until I had to admit my two-year-old sister was a more insightful conversationalist. But I was glad I dated him; I learned some skills I could put to better use with some other guy down the road. The kind of skills you have to write in code in your diary in case your mom reads it.

The memory was over.

I brushed my teeth in the bathroom (my own! Score one for England!) by the light of the 1970s big-eyed owl night-light. The wallpaper was gold foil depicting wheat stalks: so retro.

I pulled back the jade-colored bedspread and got in bed. I missed my quilt from home, a red and white thing my grandma made from a pattern in a book of Amish quilts.

I lay there looking at the ceiling, the kind of plaster that shows semicircular sweeps from some kind of tool. Like little white rainbows. I counted them. Wasn't sure if I should count the half sweeps over by the walls.

Come on, you must be tired, go ahead and sleep, I coached myself.

I was drifting restlessly when I heard the organ. It was playing low and quiet, a plodding, rhythmic bit of music, so subtle I thought for a while it was just noise in my head.

When I realized what I was hearing, I sat bolt upright, my heart pounding. The music seemed to disappear the more I concentrated on listening, like trying to figure out what a newscaster is saying on TV a room away.

I wandered out to the living room, where Steven was reading. The room was dark and he sat in the light cast by the gigantic hanging orb. Mom must have already gone to bed.

"Did you hear that?" I asked him.

His gaze didn't waver from the page. He was like that; he'd get caught up in whatever he was reading

"I thought I heard that organ playing, Steven," I said louder. "Do you think there's someone else in the house?"

He closed the book, letting it lie in his lap, and rubbed his face with both hands. Exhausted. Maybe sad. "Just forget about it," he said. "Let it go."

"Seriously? But if there's someone in the house . . ."

He sighed. He knew how to make gestures like that speak volumes. That sigh said, *You're a hysterical teenager, chill out.*

Insulted, I almost said something pissy, but I stopped myself. We had moved to England because of me. I had done something so very, very awful that we had to leave the country. If he didn't think the organ was anything to worry about, it wasn't anything to worry about.

"Okay," I said with a little smile. "They'll come for you first."

He grimaced.

I had imagined the organ because I was jet-lagged and out of sorts. Freaked out about living in a different house, a different continent. I went back down the hall-way, opening the door to my own personal scarab-green room.

I lay down on the bed and closed my eyes, but I didn't sleep. I couldn't relax enough.

CHAPTER TWO

The small town of Grenshire has no industry to boast of. Dotted with small pastures and dairies, the landscape is rural and unremarkable. The Hoffman Academy provided excellent education for boys until its closure in 1964; today's Emmons School is a coeducational facility with consistently high test scores. A privately held estate, the Arnaud Manor (built 1721–23) was the home of French émigrés and has fallen into disrepair.

—From *A History of the Towns of Northern England*

*T*he next morning, I went and sat at the breakfast table even though I wasn't hungry. Mom and Tabby were eating toast topped with butter and jelly, which Tabby managed to smear all over the lower hemisphere of her face. I listened to Tabby's charming attempts at conversation, wondering where Steven was. Mom valiantly carried on her side of the inane discussion. She had a lot of patience, I had to admit, watching her try to clean wriggling Tabby, who kept saying "Don't want."

This move sucked for Mom. She would be stuck here all day with a toddler and without any neighbors.

"Mom, I'll help you watch Tabby this summer, before I go to school," I said.

She paused and smiled tiredly. "You're going to have

the summer of your life, running around this place," she said. "Just try not to fall through a trapdoor."

"Track door," said Tabby.

"You want me to watch her now?" I asked. "You and Steven can have some time together. Go out for coffee or something."

"What would I do without you?" she said, but she made no move to transfer Tabby to my arms. Whatever. She'd complain about never having time to herself, but then not take me up on a babysitting offer. I watched her continue to coo at Tabby and decipher her stilted sentences.

Later, I went outside. It was making me nutty that there were no windows except in the living room, which faced the central courtyard. Our apartment was like a closed shoe box wedged into a large closet.

I looked up, studying the face of the manor. The stones were dark with age, and the leaded glass windows offered no curtains to soften them. I could see that this was an architectural masterpiece with turrets, towers, and lots of engineering to make the varying levels of the stories work, but it left me cold. It was basically the manor you'd like to pay an entry fee for, roam around in for an afternoon, then go home to your clean, bright, real person's home.

I continued wandering the courtyard, thinking about how things had changed in the last few years. Babies need a lot of attention, but so did I. Dealing with Richard Spees would've been easier if Mom had actually shown some interest in my first real boyfriend. Deciding to break up with him wasn't that simple, and she wasn't there for me.

If you think about it, I had basically been an only child for the first decade-plus of my life. Suddenly there was this unexpected baby that wailed all night and depleted Mom's energy with breast-feeding, and the house got filled with all these happy-colored toys that plinked out songs I could *not* get out of my head. Dinner conversations were no longer about what we'd all done that day, but instead what *Tabby* had done all day. Very little, in my opinion—but to Mom and Steven it was a freakin' marvel that she'd managed to identify the letters *a* and *b* in a police lineup.

I'm not as bitter as I sound. These years are the ones in which you're supposed to detach from your parents, right? Preparing for college and adult life, becoming independent? But it was still a surprisingly hard adjustment for me.

And if I think hard about it, maybe there was something about the fact that Steven is my stepdad, but Tabby's real father. Steven's been a great dad to me since my dad split . . . maybe I'm also mourning the loss of *his* attention. My status as his "daughter" took a blow when the real one showed up—although that's just my imagination. He still treats me like I'm his.

"Oh please, Phoebe, get a life," I said aloud.

I really, really do love Tabby, by the way.

Steven told us he'd watch Tabby while Mom and I went into town. I was glad to get off the grounds of our bleak mansion, but soon found I was in another uncomfortable situation. I had to hold my breath, biting my lip, as Mom negotiated the strangeness of steering from the other side of the car. I looked over at her, her pretty face strained, wrinkles a little more noticeable when she was stressed out. She took her hand off the wheel for a second to tuck a strand of her short hair behind her ear. I noticed that her perfectly shaped eyebrows were starting to grow in; she'd meant to wax them before we'd left the U.S.

"Aren't most people in the world right-handed?" she muttered. "Who would put a gear shift on the left?"

As soon as the road became paved and Mom got the knack of driving, I felt better. Soon we were seeing other houses, and gardens. When we hit town limits, I looked closely to see what our new "hometown" offered. It was very small, with a movie theater that listed only two movies on its marquee. I saw a few restaurants with floral half curtains, and some impressive wood-paneled structures with the strange, wonderful word *pub* on them. Somehow the British made a bar seem timeless and historic by calling it a pub.

Not many people walked these narrow streets. We saw a few middle-aged women wearing handkerchiefs over their heads and carrying string bags with their groceries inside. There weren't any parking meters on High Street, which was the town's main street. Our British car, which Steven had purchased unseen while we were still in the U.S., was one of the few vehicles at the curb after Mom parked. I saw the grocery store, a small glass-fronted shop the size of a retail store, rather than a supermarket.

We got out and started walking, looking in at quaint, dark stores. I didn't see a single person my age. I tried to ignore the sick feeling in my gut.

In four blocks, we had reached the limits of town. The shops and pubs gave way to homes. In the distance, I could see the curving roofline of a behemoth of a tall brick building, overly grand for the plainness of Grenshire. Something about it seemed familiar.

"That's the pool," said Mom. She had stopped walking and was staring at it.

She had researched Grenshire a little before we moved here. Not much, since we were in a rush, but I'd leaned over her shoulder as she searched the Web, and I remembered now that this big brick building was the pool house of the former boys' academy, now owned by the town.

"My kind of place," I said.

"Tabby will need swimming lessons eventually," she said.

"Yeah!" I said excitedly. "I'll help her learn."

"Not for a long, long time, though," she said.

"Some people start kids when they're newborn," I said. "I think you waited until I was four, though."

"Oh, Phoebe," she said, and her voice was filled with love.

I grinned. Mom and I had great memories of my learning to swim at the Y in San Francisco. We'd eat at the nearby Mediterranean hole-in-the-wall restaurant before going home. To this day, when I finish a swim I have a momentary craving for falafel and lemonade with crushed mint leaves floating in it.

"Mind if we check it out?" I asked. She turned away and I started to frown at her abrupt departure from a moment of nostalgia I wanted to linger in . . . but she rubbed her shoulder. This was her little message to me from back in the swimming-lesson days. Rather than nagging me about whether I had my duffel bag slung over my shoulder, she'd touch hers to remind me.

So I touched my shoulder now, and burst out laughing. Somehow she'd slipped my swim bag onto my shoulder without my noticing. She truly was the coolest mom. "How about just a half hour?" I asked. I doubted there was enough retail to keep her entertained in the town for longer than that.

As soon as I opened one of the glass double doors, I could smell the magic elixir: chlorine and damp towels. This was my world. Longing rushed through me. It had been forever since I last swam.

I approached the woman tending the counter in the lobby, a high-ceilinged atrium of wasted space, the kind of grand entrance builders never indulged in anymore.

"Hi," I said. "I don't have any cash on me right now. Any pounds, I mean. But I'll be buying a membership. Is it okay if I swim today?"

Toward the end of my pitiful speech, her cell phone rang and she simply nudged the pile of towels on the counter closer to me.

"Thanks!" I said. "But it's okay. I brought my own."

Although the lobby was a masterpiece, the locker room was dank.

Lined with those old-fashioned gray lockers that take padlocks (my high school got rid of lockers circa 1982 when the administration wised up to the idea of drugs) and containing a moist concrete floor gently sloping to a central drain, it looked like an asylum basement.

But when I walked out the door marked POOL, I quickly changed my mind.

Despite the morose locker room, the building's owners had obviously once had lots and lots of those pound notes with the image of a slightly worried young queen. The two-story ceiling was high above and created of tinted glass bricks, so everything had a green glow. The water rippled with the handful of people doing laps in their buoyed lanes, and a lifeguard station towered over it all like a derrick. Although I could smell the chlorine, the airiness of the structure made it so it wasn't the slap in the face an indoor pool can sometimes be.

I used the ladder and winced as I always did at the initial cold of the water. I kept moving and forced myself to submerge at the bottom, so I could start swimming and get warm. Half the pool was for free swim, and three lanes had been marked with cones for slow, medium, and fast. I dipped under the buoys and went to the fast lane. One person was already swimming there. I waited until he was at the other end before starting, so we wouldn't lap each other.

I adjusted my goggles and pushed off, with a wave of

relief that was so tangible it broke my heart. *Oh, dear water, you are my savior,* I thought. With my body doing its mechanical, happy thing, my mind was able to sink into a blue-green haze and release my stress over our sinister mansion and whatever I'd done to get us there.

My arms pulled overhead, forcefully pushing water behind me as I outswam my furiously churning mind. The rhythm of waiting to take a breath, counting to do so, let me relax in a way nothing else does. Arms moving, legs kicking firmly, my hips slipping like an eel through the water, tilting my head to take that breath when I needed it, my ear catching the muffled buzz through my swim cap of the world above the pool . . . I could almost burst with how good it felt.

It took a while for me to even notice the guy in the lane—he had been a flicker every few minutes as we passed each other mid-pool, just someone to avoid bumping into. But when we next drew up level, facing different directions, I'd reached the Zen point where I could begin to accept other input, so I checked him out. He was *fine*. I couldn't see his face too well because he wore goggles, too, but he had nice thick black wavy hair and a long, muscular body.

I continued swimming, but now I was anticipating each time we passed, sucking in my stomach even though I knew he couldn't see it through the spume of kicked water. But I had to laugh at myself. It's impossible to look good while you're swimming. Your mouth is doing funny stuff as you fight for that breath, your eyes are hidden behind the goggles, and your head is encased in black rubber. Not the best look.

I finished my laps, then moved into the free-swim area to tread water and stretch into my cooldown. I turned my head to look for him still swimming back there—but he wasn't in the lane. He had followed me.

Close enough to touch, he treaded water. He had an amazing head, strong jawline and ruddy cheeks, with that great jet-black hair. His shoulders were massive and muscled—but unlike most jocks, his neck was not a football player's stubby trunk, but instead was graceful and long. This was all I could see of him through the goggles and water, and it was very impressive. He grinned at me and I smiled back, hoping my nose wasn't running like it sometimes did after a swim.

"You've got a great stroke," he said in a totally charming English accent.

I bit my lip to not laugh. My mind's not always in the gutter, but c'mon, a great stroke? Maybe it didn't mean the same thing to British guys.

"Thanks," I said. "You, too!"

"Oh, you're an American."

I nodded. "My family just moved here. From California."

"Brilliant. Then you can be on our swim team!" He looked truly excited about the idea, even through the dark blue of his goggles. That reminded me; I could take mine off. I slid them up to prop them on my swim cap. I thought it would look way too vain to take the cap off, a little too much like those romance novels where the heroine shakes her hair out of its bun. As soon as I had done it, though, I remembered that these goggles left red furrows around my eyes. Great. Now I looked like a sleep-deprived raccoon.

But he did the same thing—somehow he had avoided the red mark of goggle suction—and now I had a chance to see his beautiful sapphire blue eyes, with the dark lashes and eyebrows that were just the right amount of tufty. If you had asked me to describe the kind of guy I found most attractive, I could have just pointed to him and saved myself the trouble of explaining.

"Sure," I said. "I was on the swim team at home."

"It'll be brilliant to have you. Our lads go to the championship every year, but the females have been a little worse for wear. You're *fast*. You'll be head of team, no doubt, from what I just saw."

I grinned. Finally, something was going right for me in Grenshire. "Do you have a good coach?"

"Yeah. It's just the sorry luck of the draw that we haven't had a strong girls' team."

I continued treading water, feeling my heart rate slow back down.

"What's your name?" he asked.

"Phoebe Irving."

"I'm Miles Whittleby." He extended his hand and we shook formally, lurching a little in the water.

"What's school like?" I asked.

"It's all right," he said. "The usual collection of the clueless and the gifted, and everything in between."

"Are your friends all on swim team, too?"

"No, I'm the only one. They're more into athletics . . . I think you call it 'track and field.' And a few play in the band."

"That's cool," I said. "I always wanted to play an instrument."

"Yeah, one plays violin and the other the oboe."

"Are you musical at all?" I asked.

"No, just a listener. And don't even ask me about dancing."

I burst out into a peal of laughter. "I'm sure you're fine," I teased.

"No, it's an abomination. People have injured their eyes watching."

"It can't be that bad!"

"Oh, worse. At dances I tend to huddle against the wall to spare everyone."

"Well, no fear, I'll huddle with you." As soon as I said it, I could have hit myself. What a lame thing to say . . . and so presumptuous. But he didn't react like it was either.

"Perfect! Another convert to the 'let's *not* dance' club. David Bowie hates us."

I smiled, relieved at his response. "Actually, I do kind of like to dance."

"Maybe I can just shuffle my feet back and forth when no one's looking."

"Sounds elegant."

"And do the macarena," he added.

"Um . . ."

He burst out laughing.

"Okay, okay!" I said. "I wasn't sure if you were joking."

"I'll introduce you to my friends," he said. "They'll like you. I imagine the first day of school can be hard when you don't know anyone?"

"I've never done it," I admitted. Under the water, I clenched my hands in excitement. Things had just become easier. He was going to set me up with people who would most likely be my friends from now on. And a chance to keep hanging out with *him*? Über magnifico, as German Italians say. Or as Orwell would put it, doubleplusgood.

"It'll be fine. We can get together beforehand, so you'll know some of them."

"Thank you," I said. "That's huge. I was a little nervous about the whole thing."

"No worries," he said. "So where do you live?"

"This really old place that's been in the family for a while. My stepdad's family, I mean. The Arnaud Manor."

His mouth opened, then he closed it with a shudder. "You live *there*?"

"My stepdad couldn't sell it and we had to move anyway, so this was where we ended up. Wait, what?"

He had muttered something after I said, "couldn't sell it."

"Nothing," he said.

"No, really, what'd you say?"

He dipped his head backward in the water and got his hair wet again. It was sexy but also sort of self-conscious.

"Sorry," he said. "I didn't mean to insult you or your family. I said, 'what a shocker.' "

"I know what you mean," I said, trying to figure out if I should feel offended. "It's been neglected."

"Neglected. And haunted."

"Uh . . . what?" I asked.

"There's the small matter of the undead woman who drinks blood. That tends to inhibit sales."

"*What?*"

"No one told you about Madame Arnaud?"

"No."

"She's the one who built the house and supposedly still lives there. She's immortal from drinking blood."

"*Whose* blood?"

"Children's blood."

"You've got to be kidding me."

"It's the local legend," he said.

I wondered briefly if Steven knew the crazy rumors about the manor. I stared up into the mossy green glass of the faraway ceiling, trying to figure out how to respond.

Was Miles messing with me? Maybe he'd made it up on the spot. I'd always loved reading ghost stories, but that was because they had nothing to do with real life.

I looked at him uneasily. He just waited, a half smile playing on his plum-colored lips.

Finally I said, "*You* don't believe it, do you?"

CHAPTER THREE

Employment prospects for gardeners, groomsmen, smiths,
and all manner of servants of the interior.
Enquire at Arnaud Manor, service door of the west wing.

—*Grenshire Argus*, October 5, 1721

"Show yourself," I said aloud. I was in the old part of the manor near the mouth of the gargantuan fireplace. A damp smell blew down through the network of chimneys. Dust motes swirled around like bacteria in a petri dish.

After we came home, Mom went to lie down, taking a nap at the same time as Tabby. Steven was working on his laptop. I considered asking him if I could go into the old part of the house, but Bethany taught me that it's easier to ask for forgiveness than permission.

So I had crept out the door and into the mottled sunshine, marching across the dirt to the official entrance to the manor. I had put the key in the screaming mouth, opened the heavy door, and entered.

Now I stood dwarfed by the enormous stones of the great hall. Trailing up to the ceiling like a bad idea was the grandiose staircase. I inhaled the ferment and automatically found myself slowing into my lap-swimming breathing pattern.

I went upstairs and soon was opening the thick wooden door to the library, staring up at the rows and rows of shelves. Miles's words flickered through my mind. A woman who drank blood for centuries, giving the manor a reputation akin to Castle Dracula. A village that turned a blind eye to her evil, too frightened to intervene.

Just on a whim, I pulled one book out at eye level. It had a French title, and inside were etchings of horses performing some kind of patterned dance. As I looked at its place on the shelf to put it back, I saw instead of wood . . . glass. It was a tiny window.

I pulled several more books off the shelf, letting them drop to the floor. The window wasn't very much wider than a few thick volumes' spines, though. I pressed myself closer so I could peer through it.

On the other side, I could see another room, which held a cot and a trunk. It was barely the size of a closet. I couldn't imagine a more bleak room. In many haunted house movies, the bookcase revolves to reveal a secret passageway. I looked around for whatever lever might activate it, so it would swing open to show a cackling Vincent Price holding a candelabra on the other side. I started pulling books down again, looking for a door-knob or switch.

In the end, the case didn't revolve. Instead, a little door was concealed within the larger bookshelf, and the books swung with the door, just like a robe hung from a hook on the bathroom door. I hadn't needed to take down all those books after all, and in fact their position on the floor blocked the door from completely opening. I took five minutes to put them back.

The door was heavy with all the books back on the shelves, held up by iron brackets painted to look like books, but I threw my hip into it until it creaked open wide enough for me. I opened it even more because if the weight of the books made it creep closed while I was inside, well . . . that would suck.

I went in.

The room was oppressively tiny, like a fairy's cottage. I raised my hand and laid it flat along the low ceiling, bringing down a stream of dust. I walked over to the iron cot that was covered in a patchwork quilt with lots of hand-tied knots. If possible, it seemed smaller than a twin bed. Who had had to sleep here?

I knelt on the floor to open the trunk. Its surprisingly heavy lid creaked. I stared inside at the network of cubbies. Rather than one big empty space, as I'd imagined those large trunks would hold, it was divided into little sections and drawers, all covered in peeling rosebud wallpaper. Poking around, I saw old-fashioned underthings in plain white muslin and lots of heavy black dresses. In the last place I looked, I found floor-length white aprons. Of course! Only a maid would sleep in a room this small.

I stood, holding one of the aprons to my chest. I was about to hook the ties around my neck, but instead let it drop to the floor, my fingers trembling.

I took two steps to reach the window to the outside. I pulled aside the gauzy curtain, thick with gray debris— and saw the long plunge down to the ground. But something embedded in the glass itself caught my eye. I rubbed my fingers against the window until a circle of clean glass showed through. Someone had etched a message.

I shook my head. No, I wasn't seeing this.

The poor little babes, it said, in very old-fashioned writing.

It seemed to be evidence for what Miles had said, that Madame Arnaud drank children's blood. But I didn't want to believe it. I began thinking furiously, trying to craft different reasons for a maid to scratch this particular message into the glass. Her own miscarriages?

In the corner of the window, something began moving, and I saw that it was Mom, outside walking the courtyard with Tabitha on her hip. Tabby was wearing a blue seersucker dress, and pulling at Mom's hair. I can't describe how surreal that felt, stuck in the heart of that dark stone house, and seeing the two of them out there, smiling.

I tried to open the window, but it didn't budge. I began to panic, for no good reason. The house wasn't on fire, and I wasn't trying to cast myself out of the window. It didn't matter that it wasn't opening.

Below me, winding up the booky staircase from down

the hall, came one note from the organ. A brief sound, almost ignorable.

But to make sound come from the organ, someone had to pump the foot pedals first. It would never utter a whisper by itself—a boulder could fall on the keys and they would sink down soundlessly.

I froze, my heart racing. "Steven?" I called.

He must have noticed the door key was gone and followed me in, and was playing the organ to let me know the jig was up.

"Steven?" I yelled again, at the top of my lungs.

Too loud, don't make the house angry.

No answer.

My body flooded with adrenaline, my heart feeling three sizes larger and flailing around in my chest like an out-of-control animal. The servant's room had trapped me.

No one knew I was here. The mansion's size meant no one would hear me screaming. I was completely vulnerable to whoever was playing the organ.

The only way out was back through the ballroom . . . where the organ's player waited. I looked around the miniature room frantically—was there any kind of weapon? I pulled the house key from my pocket; although it was huge it was dull.

I tried to quiet my panting breath and listen.

The mansion was quiet . . . too quiet. It felt like it was listening to *me*.

I looked at the open bookcase door, wanting to push

it closed, keeping me hidden in the maid's room. But I couldn't remember if it squeaked.

I crept toward it. If the person had hunted me into the library, my movement would be detected. I'd have to close the door quickly and absolutely silently. Thank God I had put back all the books on the other side, or the sprawl of books in front of the shelf would be a giveaway.

I sucked in a deep breath as I began to ease the door closed, just like I was taught in photography class: to be absolutely still, inhale while taking a picture.

The door creaked.

So loudly that I cringed. Still, I wedged the door closed and sank down to the floor with my back against it.

It's okay, I tried to tell myself. *It wasn't as loud as you think. And how could they track it back to this door—it's closed now. If they don't know about it, you're safe.*

I carefully looked up—even my hair rustling against the door sounded loud—toward the window in the door. I couldn't see it from this vantage point, which meant that I couldn't be seen, either.

I listened . . . I waited.

I looked at my wrist to see what time it was. No watch there. But eventually Mom and Steven would miss me and come looking. There was nowhere else to go on this monstrous estate except here . . . I just had to wait. They'd come get me. They would. Right? Unless they thought I was outside and started combing the woods. Oh God, that would take hours. Days.

I'm here, I'm here, I tried to mentally tell them.

And who was *there*? Madame Arnaud looking for another child to taste?

Or . . . this house had been empty so long. Maybe someone had taken up residence. Someone who was supposed to be taking medications to control their mental disease, but failed to. Someone crazed and violent.

Someone who would bludgeon Steven with a baseball bat when he came to find me. Someone who would kill me, too, when I heard Steven's screams and rushed out to help. And after he'd eviscerated both of us, he'd go into the modern, clean apartment and take care of Mom and Tabby.

All four of our bodies gelling and cooling in the mansion . . . who would miss us? Maybe in the fall someone from the school would call, if Mom had already registered me. The police would come and find us glued to the floor by our own decomposing. We'd be morbid headlines.

I waited. I listened, listened, listened.

A lot of time passed. My mind wandered; I thought about Bethany. I eventually yawned.

Maybe there *was* a way for the organ to play without someone pumping the pedals. Maybe a mouse was inside the works, applying his rodent teeth to tubing that somehow emitted a mild sound upon puncture.

I yawned again. My heart had long ago slowed: that wild beast in my chest had its head tucked into its paws, sleeping.

I was stiff from sitting so long, so I carefully began

moving my limbs and rolling my neck around. I waited probably another twenty minutes, then I stood up, dusted off my jeans, and opened the bookshelf door.

I listened again, carefully, looking into the vast depths of that gigantic library. I closed the door behind me, and began going back down the staircase, stealthily, just to be sure. I reached the floor and walked over to the door to the hallway leading to the ballroom.

Oh my God.

No.

I hadn't closed this door—and it was closed now.

I backed away from it. I had to return to the secrecy of the servant's room. That was my only chance. I took a few steps backwards, just a few . . . when something insane, totally insane, happened.

The library completely vanished.

Instead, I was in the ballroom, facing the organ, five feet in front of me. A woman sat on its bench, her back to me. She wore a rotted silk dress, her right arm extended to the side. Where the fabric had torn, decayed skin revealed the muscles underneath. Her right index finger had decomposed so much that just one long bone stuck out at the end. That bone was still resting on the organ key she had played about an hour ago.

Silently, she turned her head around. She had dark hair, but I couldn't see what her face was like since it was so undone by time. She had high cheekbones that shone through the frayed parchment of her skin.

A little smile played on her worm-destroyed lips, as she held my gaze. She stood up.

Like a parishioner making her way out of the pew after church, she walked sideways to free herself and her
voluminous skirts off the bench. She turned, all the while
watching me. She took a slow step toward me, gracefully,
although so terribly *wrong* with her skirts falling apart and
her face peeling as if she'd been horribly sunburned
rather than having lived for many centuries.

She was coming to me.

I had to move. But this was a *vision*. I was there with
my mind, not my body.

She took another step. Two more, and she would be
able to touch me. I *willed* myself to move, and managed
a single step backward. Relief flooded through me; I
could escape, I could get the hell out of here. The exit
was to my right, so I shifted my weight to that foot and
began taking steady steps. I still couldn't force myself to
run, but I was going faster than she was in her stately pur-
suit, as her frail cloth slippers took step after step.

It was the slowest, dripped-in-syrup hunt, and every
step I took required intense will from me, incredible energy. In my peripheral vision, I saw I was approaching
the door. Maybe once I stepped through its threshold her
strange lock on me would be broken and I could *run*.

I thought my way carefully through each backward
step. I counted the black-and-white parquet squares between us. She extended her hand to me, half flesh and
half bone, as if beseeching me to stop. But I was so close,
so close, so close. There was the door, the rounded stones
in an arch, and then I was through it.

I could sense the grand staircase behind me, but I

couldn't take my eyes off her. If I looked away, maybe she'd blurt forward like a rabbit. To keep her slow, I had to watch her. The floor changed under my feet to the stone tablets of the grand entryway. I kept going. Now I could see the balustrade. I would have to go down backward, watching her. I could clutch the banister and use it to guide me down the stairs.

I was there, I was there, I could feel the slight breeze drifting up from the front door open far below me. She shook her head at me.

Instantly the vision ended, and I was back in the library looking at the closed door.

I screamed.

The doorknob turned.

The ornate, oval golden knob slowly spun.

The door flung open and crashed against the wall. The woman wasn't there, but I heard a small moan in my ear, and cold air passed through my hair. The presence was behind me, so I ran forward, down the short hall, into the ballroom.

The organ began playing a complex song with half notes and quarter notes in a rapid volley, a virtuoso performance to mock my flight down the sharp, wicked stairs. It was as if the organ knew I had been trying to convince myself I hadn't heard it, and was rolling out its most deafening and grandiose performance.

As soon as I got outside, the organ stopped mid-tune.

Silence. Except . . . from far away, the faintest hint of a laugh.

CHAPTER FOUR

Paranoid delusions, with the idea that someone is watching you
or stalking you, can be a big part of schizophrenia.

—Class presentation excerpt,
Bethany Robb and Phoebe Irving

I tore into the apartment, making little half-breath screams. They were in the kitchen, all three of them. Mom was chopping something while Steven entertained Tabby at the table.

"There's a ghost," I shrieked. "She's living in the house and she's your ancestor, Steven, and she drank blood, and she . . ."

I went on and on, sobbing. I told them everything I'd seen—and what Miles had told me. Mom finished her chopping and came to sit at the table, staring at Tabby, this kind of grieved expression on her face. Clearly she didn't want Tabby to hear it and get scared. She just wanted me to shut up so she could pay attention to the kid that *did* matter.

Steven looked at me only once, then his gaze flickered back to Tabby.

It was always this way. When I'd told them about fainting over Richard Spees, Mom had actually laughed. "You sure know how to work yourself up," she'd said at the time, and her face said the same thing now.

I felt a rush of frustration and rage, my cheeks flaming. Why didn't they *listen* to me? Because it was my fault we were here?

Mom used to listen to me, used to lay her cheek against mine and sit quietly while I told her things. Even when I was big, she'd pull me onto her lap and wrap her arms around me from behind. But that was before Tabby was born.

"You guys are just evil!" I said. "You don't—"

Before I could finish the sentence, something awful happened. Something wrenched me out of that kitchen and whistled me through time . . . *backward*.

I wound up back in California, a year or so ago, back in the same discussion I had been thinking about. The conversation about my fainting.

My breath halted in my throat.

What was going on?

Mom and Steven didn't react. To them, it was as if this were happening for the first time. They had the same expressions. Mom was wearing the Allo Oiseau dress she'd bought at the designer's rack sale, and her hair was falling out of her clip as she lightly scolded me.

"Maybe you should think about *why* this happened to you," she was saying.

What? Why I had just traveled through time to this weird memory?

No. I put my hands over my face. She meant I should think about why a fainting spell happened to me.

Panic welled up in me. Surely I was still in the Arnaud kitchen, telling them about Madame Arnaud? But this was San Francisco, with our sunny kitchen window giving a view of the backyard eucalyptus tree sloughing off its aromatic bark. I couldn't understand why I was stuck in some old, totally unimportant memory.

"We need to leave," I pleaded.

". . . need to take better care of yourself, Phoebe," Steven was saying. "What did you have for lunch?"

The words came automatically to my mouth, although I wanted to talk about Madame Arnaud, and not what I'd eaten so long ago. "I bought a Caesar salad, but what does that have to do with anything?"

"You're not eating well," Mom agreed. "It's easy to get light-headed if you're just eating lettuce."

"Have chicken on it next time," said Steven. "You're an athlete; you're burning calories."

"And remember to breathe," Mom teased, "when you're talking to a boy."

I felt helpless. The fainting had nothing to do with food, with excitement. It was something my body did inexplicably. *Listen to me,* I tried to say, but Tabby derailed everything, like she did then, like she was doing now . . .

She had tried to get out of her chair and fallen, hitting her forehead on the table edge. Now she was crying wildly, while Steven hugged her and Mom leaned across the table with her arms extended, so he could hand her over.

Time skipped again while she leaned.

Her Allo Oiseau dress morphed into the simple red Old Navy sweatshirt she was wearing on top of jeans. The bright sunlight faded. The table was no longer our blond wood one that she and Steven had put on their wedding registry; it was now the dark oak of the Arnaud kitchen's. I was back. We were all back.

Steven handed Tabby to Mom. She soothed her youngest daughter with new words: words that hadn't come from previous conversations, from a different country.

I sank down into a chair opposite Steven. I was going crazy. I must have just had a psychotic episode. A memory had taken me by the throat and yanked me back to the past, while the present had become filmy, stepsister to the real.

What had happened here in the last ten minutes was just as terrifying as what had happened—if it did—with Madame Arnaud. I was losing my mind. I was losing my freaking mind.

Reeling, I watched them continue their everyday talk. And after I'd made sure the present was *staying,* and I wasn't going to shift somewhere else, I rose and went quietly back to my lime green bedroom.

I lay down on the bed without pulling back the covers. What was the use? I knew I wouldn't be able to sleep anyway.

I rolled over onto my side and a paper in my pocket crinkled. Wiggling around a little, I was able to pull it out.

I read it while a headache built fortifications in my skull. Soon my head was throbbing as I stared at Bethany's careful handwriting, once so familiar to me. This was an explanation for what I'd seen in the old part of the manor . . . and for what had just happened in the kitchen. It made perfect sense.

The paper was a page from her notebook, notes she'd started to take for our presentation in psychology class. We hadn't gotten far, and that night we couldn't find this page, so we'd started over again on her laptop. I guess I hadn't worn these pants since then. Mom had packed them for me, not knowing I didn't like the way the waist sat.

The headache drove a mallet into my brain again and again.

I read the page a hundred times.

And then I read it again.

Schizophrenia Presentation
by Bethany Robb and Phoebe Irving
  I. Schizophrenia can show up in kids as young as
    5, but it's more typical for it to show up in the
    teen years
  II. Some of the positive symptoms (explain)
    include:
    A. Auditory hallucinations—hearing things like
      voices that aren't there
    B. Visual hallucinations—seeing things

C. *Either being unable to sleep, or sleeping way
too much*
D. *A fierce belief that the hallucinations are
real*
E. *Garbled speech or thought*
III. *Some of the*

I was swimming. Miles wasn't there and I couldn't see anyone else, either. The pool was dark and silent, no splashing sounds. The lighting was so dim I forced myself to relax into it, absorbed by the familiar sensations of my body threading the water's needle.

I don't know how long this lasted. Hours, maybe. Then the lights came on and someone entered, setting up cones for the lanes. Shortly afterward, children trickled in and took a swim class from the lifeguard who'd opened the pool up.

I treaded water and watched them for a long time, remembering my first lessons and how initially I'd been terrified to put my face in the water. Their serious faces were so heartbreaking as they kicked their stubby legs and swam back to their mothers. The class ended. The high ceiling echoed with their talk as they headed back to the locker room, and the pool settled.

I was alone again, a single flower in a dark blue field. Free swim began and I pulled myself out to make room in the lane for those lean-bodied adults who came, swam steadily, then toweled off and left.

I stayed forever, watching swimmers come and go. None of them were Miles. I had to admit that was why

I'd lingered, although I couldn't remember when I'd asked Mom to come pick me up. Or maybe they'd lent me the car? No: I would've remembered my first time driving on the left side of the road.

You're losing your grip again, I thought, and shivered. Which reminded me I'd never dried off, sitting there dripping on the cold tile.

I stood and stretched. Miles wasn't coming.

I walked into the kitchen and they were all eating dinner. *Oh crap.* Setting the table was my job. Mom must've called me and I didn't hear her . . . and in these post-screw-up days, I wasn't given extra chances. She had set the table and deliberately didn't set a place for me.

"I'm really sorry, I didn't hear you calling me," I said.

Mom said nothing, just swabbed at some applesauce Tabby had pushed over the edge of her plastic bunny plate.

"I feel like a jerk," I said. "I didn't mean to forget my job."

"I'll set the table from now on," said Steven.

"No!" I said. "I can do it. I honestly didn't hear you. The acoustics here are really weird."

"Oh, Steven," said Mom. "That's sweet of you. One less thing to . . ." Her voice drifted off.

"Seriously! It's not a big deal. I just didn't hear you!" I protested.

They were studiously ignoring me. Such is the fate of the teen who has let down her family. My eyes filled with tears, and I turned around and went back to my room. I wasn't hungry. I didn't need dinnertime chatter. I sat on my bed and imagined a window where no window existed: I let curtains billow in a breeze and send the fragrance of roses to me. I calmed. I didn't even end up crying. I would just have to make a better effort from now on. Try harder.

Nighttime.

Tabby woke up crying and I listened through the wall as Mom went in and changed her diaper and sang her one more lullaby.

I'd been awake for hours, thinking about what I'd experienced: seeing Madame Arnaud although I knew I hadn't, spending hours at the pool in a weird daze. Even the simple example of forgetting to set the table.

They had meds for this kind of thing. I could ask Mom to make me an appointment. I'd be assertive with her, and I wouldn't let Tabby get in the way of saying what I needed to. This time I'd be completely clear, and I wouldn't let anything divert me from talking to her. *I need to see someone,* I'd say. *A therapist. I'm seeing things, Mom.*

I wished I could call Bethany, but I hadn't charged my cell and it was dead. She'd be cycling through Web pages to find me the best therapist, and the whole time she'd be babbling and laughing so I wouldn't feel bad. "You know, you didn't have to develop schizophrenia just because we did a report on it," she'd tease. "I know you're super scholarly, but no one expects that."

I stretched out on my bed, feeling an ache for her and

for my life back in California. Everything was *light* back there. England didn't even offer windows.

I kept mentally rehearsing what I'd say to Mom. *I just don't feel right, and I think I need help.* I imagined the look on Mom's face as she tried to process the idea that her daughter had mental issues. In my vision, her face instantly relaxed as Tabby came up and hugged her legs. She bent, picked her up, and asked her if she was hungry. *No!* I shouted in my imagination. *Listen to me! Listen to me for once! I need help!*

I'd tell her in the morning.

Why wait? I imagined Bethany saying. She was right. Based on the silence from the room next door, Tabby was back asleep and Mom had left. I got off the bed and left my room, walking past Tabby's room where she slept, kneeling with her butt in the air, the puffiness of her diaper making her body look like a loaf of bread. I smiled in at her. She was a good kid. It wasn't her fault she got all the attention.

I continued down the hallway and turned the corner.

Panic stabbed my brain. I tried to scream but all I managed was a raw sob.

Madame Arnaud blocked my way. This time she was pretty, with porcelain skin and dark black hair. But somehow her beauty was worse than seeing her real self, more deceptive and conniving. I could dimly hear the television from the living room. Mom and Steven were close by but completely unaware.

Madame Arnaud's carmine skirts were as wide as the hall, and the embroidery on her bodice was dazzlingly elaborate. She exuded wealth. She was a bold, pestilent velvet blotch, her pallor kin to the porcelain-colored walls. I tried to back away, but couldn't.

As she walked toward me, her hair moved slightly; a nest of spiders seethed in her coiffure. One of the larger spiders crawled out of her hair and down her forehead, its legs slow and solid as it crossed the plane of her pale brow. It resembled a beauty spot, like the ones French nobles pasted onto their cheeks, but this one was alive. She didn't notice.

I tried to scream, tried to move, but I was frozen. The hall filled with the sound of my heartbeat. It seemed like the walls trembled to the sound, my pulse dictating the way the house throbbed.

She's not there, I told myself. *You need medication. You're hallucinating.*

She stopped and stared at me. My heart skipped a beat, and so did the walls, lurching after a delayed second.

Her eyes widened in recognition and hatred.

She knows me? She doesn't know me. Wake the hell up.

She lifted her lip in a sneer. I imagined that to her I was a commoner worth no more than a maggot that has surged to the forefront of its popping, headless cousins.

The hallway was still pulsing with my heart, a cavernous ache pounding in my head. *She isn't there, Phoebe.*

She lifted a thin wrist dripping with diamond bracelets, and pointed behind me down the hall. I obeyed. Released from my paralysis, I backed up around the corner until I couldn't see her anymore. But I heard her skirts rustle. She was following to make sure I did what she bade.

She's in our part of the house. She betrayed some vital rule . . . she was supposed to stay only in her realm, the cob-webbed, dank, stone-walled part.

There are no rules! I screamed in my head. *She doesn't exist!*

I continued backing up, hearing those skirts from around the corner. I wasn't imagining the sound. She was taking slow, paced steps in her profusion of silk skirts. I saw the halfway open door of Tabby's room come back into my peripheral vision.

My God. Tabby.

We were isolated at the end of this hallway, my sister and I. Madame Arnaud stood between us and our parents. *Try to scream! Just do it!*

I slipped inside. Tabby's sleeping form, breathing heavily, lay humped in the crib. The night-light gave off an intimate glow, made the room a stage set for a quiet lover's confession. Her crib created a massive shadow of bars on the wall.

I heard those skirts, those whispering skirts, turning the corner.

I clung to the crib rails. *I'll protect you,* I promised in my head, but I knew I had no power.

Tabby's face was buried in darkness, and I saw the new shadow on the wall, blocking the pattern of the crib. Silk rustled behind me. I fell to my knees.

Chapter Five

Dozens of masons and hundreds of laborers worked two years on the manor's construction. A parade of carriages carried the workers back and forth each sunrise and sunset, as idiosyncrasies of the property owners did not sanction the customary temporary-workers' village. Glaziers sailed from the continent to fashion the splendid glasswork features, such as a conservatory and a rooftop tower. Tremendous efforts went into the expansive and verdant lawns, with delightfully formed topiaries, gushing fountains, and statuary to rival the finest estates close or far-flung.

—From *England: Her Cities, Her Towns, Her Pride,* Vol. XII

I still knelt on Tabby's floor. Hours had passed. I hadn't slept, but I'd been in some kind of paralyzed state. There had been a shadow show on the wall, as Madame Arnaud did whatever she did, but I sent my mind somewhere else and ignored the slow silhouette.

I hadn't been able to do a damn thing to help my sister.

My body had not belonged to me.

I had sat helpless in its husk.

Now sensation returned and I lifted myself to standing. Walked to the crib and stared down at the still-breathing soul there. Thank God.

Thank God, thank God, thank God, thank God.

Thank you, God, and I'll try harder next time, I won't let the magic freeze me, I'll fight, I'll fight her off, I'll keep my little sister safe, I'll . . .

I don't know how I could have done anything different.

I jumped, startled, when Tabby erupted into a hiccupping cry. This was her way of letting Mom know each morning that she was awake. Her eyes opened for a second, but her eyelids came down again to cover them as she sobbed.

"I'm so sorry, Tabby," I said to her. "I *tried.*"

Mom came bustling into the room, cooing, agitated, "Sweetie, it's okay, it's okay."

"Hi, Mom," I said miserably.

"Good morning, darling."

As soon as Tabby was in Mom's arms, she stopped crying. Mom carried her over to the changing table to change her diaper, throwing the wet one in the trash with a heavy thwack. It seemed like a perfectly normal morning. Mom squirted antibiotic cleanser on her hands, then wheeled around to set Tabby on the floor. Together they went to the dresser to pick out her outfit for the day.

"Mom, I have to tell you something . . ." My voice was so soft she didn't hear me over the loud squeal of the dresser drawer grinding open.

"Ow!" said Mom. She flicked her hand back and forth furiously, and paused to peel off the remnants of a broken nail. "That's what you get with a dresser that's sat for decades warping and swelling."

"Okay, Mama?" asked Tabby.

"Yes, yes," said Mom. "Things could be far worse."

Oh yes, Mom, far worse indeed. But I held my tongue, ashamed. I'd done nothing to help Tabby . . . and Mom wouldn't believe me anyway. She'd scorned me when I'd tried to tell her about Madame Arnaud before.

"I have a boo-boo, too," said Tabby.

"Let me see," said Mom. Tabby pulled up the sleeve of her Dora the Explorer pajamas to show the fairly deep puncture wound on her arm, surrounded by brown-blue bruising.

Unreal.

"My God!" said Mom. "How'd you do that? A nail on this goddamn crib?" She kissed the wound and instantly began investigating the crib for an exposed nail.

But I stayed crouched next to Tabby, staring into her eyes, terrified. "It was her, wasn't it?" I asked. While I'd crashed onto the floor in a faint or whatever it was, she'd hurt my sister somehow. I was *right there,* powerless.

"I should have gone over everything," said Mom. She sounded on the verge of tears.

"It was Madame Arnaud," I said. Mom continued to run her hands up and down the slats of the crib.

The wound was horrible, a strangely adult sight on such pristine skin. Tabby had never been blemished by anything. She was still too young for scraped knees and the assorted injuries of childhood. Cradle cap was about the worst thing her skin had ever experienced.

"I'm so sorry," I whispered to my little sister. "This is my fault. I should have fought harder."

Mom muttered to herself, as she kept looking the crib over. She even pulled out the mattress to look underneath, as if Tabby had the strength to lift a mattress her weight rested on.

"It's not the crib," I said. "Stop looking. Listen to me. It's Madame Arnaud."

I followed her hurried stride to the master bedroom, as Tabby did, where she rooted around for some Neosporin in her still-unpacked carry-on. "We'll have to find you a pediatrician here," she said as she slathered it on Tabby's arm. "Thankfully, I know you're up to date on your tetanus shot."

"Tell her, Tabby," I urged. "A woman came in big, red skirts, right?"

But Tabby was absorbed in the Band-Aid Mom was putting on her.

"Tell her, Tabby!" I shouted. Was it just my imagination that nothing I said ever got heard?

Tabby asked for another Band-Aid and Mom put it on her other arm, a mirror, a bit of symmetry.

"Tell her!" I screamed at the top of my lungs.

And then I got it.

This wasn't happening. I was in another hallucination: auditory, visual. Who knew where I really was: Asleep in my bed? Under supervision in a psychiatric hospital? Maybe the whole move to England was a long, extended delusion.

"I see," I whispered to Mom, to Tabby, involved now in layering Band-Aids in cross-hatch patterns. "It's okay. You don't have to listen to me."

★   ★   ★

Bethany had been the one to tell me about automatic writing, this thing they did in the 1800s that was kind of like Ouija, only without the laborious spelling out of every word. Basically, you sit with pen and paper and invoke a spirit . . . you invite them to use your body, and while you're in a trance, they write their messages as fast as they can.

Maybe it was a dangerous thing to do, to offer the dead the chance to borrow your body. A ghost might refuse to stop writing, and take up permanent residence in the furiously scratching—and alive—body.

Nonetheless, I headed for the den off the kitchen. Steven had set up his computer there, so I figured I could grab paper from his printer. I walked in, attracted to the sight of the giant desk with its warren of pigeonholes. I'd always wanted a desk like this, with a place for each and every secret. On the top, Steven had shoved a bunch of pens into the Yewscope mug he'd brought from home, to serve as a pencil cup. Yewscope's logo was a yew tree whose roots were flexible minicams. This was the company he worked for, headquartered in San Francisco.

Which pen to take?

It seemed like a big decision. It couldn't be just any pen. I hovered, looking at the Stabilos and uni-balls and simple BICs. Steven was a pen geek like me, so there were a lot of options. Calligraphy pens, even.

Pick one, already.

But I couldn't. It was so weird. I just stood there looking at them as though I were choosing which of several children would be permitted to live, and which would go to the ovens.

"Madame Arnaud, are you real or not?" I whispered up to the echoing ceiling.

I listened closely but the house brought no response.

I took a step closer to the pencil cup. I really needed to just grab one without thinking. It didn't matter. *A pen, Phoebe, any pen.*

"You can use my hand," I said to the air. "You can write whatever you want."

Why was I paralyzed? I looked behind me. I thought, *I should close the door behind me.* If Mom or Steven interrupted me while I was in the trance of automatic writing, it might startle my own spirit away permanently. I wanted to be able to get back inside when Madame Arnaud was done writing. I walked to the door and closed it.

Okay, time to start writing.

I'd aced Mr. Pelkey's creative writing class, and he was always reading my stuff out loud to the class without saying it was mine. I think everyone assumed he was reading different people's stories and poems each time, but he read only mine. He always wrote nice, complimentary stuff on the papers and one time wrote something for me to take home to my parents, telling them he thought I had genuine talent. That was nice to hear, and Mom and Steven had been impressed.

A memory.

I'd written a sad story, about a girl who can't relate to anybody and gets sadder and sadder throughout the story.

The last scene has her standing for hours in the attic holding a length of rope. I never explicitly came out and said it, but the idea was that she was deciding whether to hang herself.

Mr. Pelkey had asked me to stay after class, and although I was supposed to be in trig at the other end of campus, I nodded and waited for everyone else to file out.

He sat me down at his big metal desk covered with piles of student stories, and essays since he was an English teacher, too, and asked me all these uncomfortable questions about my main character.

"She seems so real," he'd said. "I was wondering how you'd known how to write the emotions and thoughts of someone so unhappy."

"I don't know," I said. His face looked way too serious.

"Did you base your character on anyone in real life?"

"No," I said. "I don't think so." Down the hall I could hear all the doors closing, as teachers started up their classes. I started to worry about trig, because sometimes we had a pop quiz right when we walked in. But Mr. Pelkey didn't seem to be in a hurry; apparently he had this next period free.

"Do you feel lonely like your character?" he asked. Behind his glasses, his ginger-colored eyebrows were raised in concern. A whole network of lines appeared on his forehead from this expression.

"Not really," I said. "She's just someone I made up."

I was sitting on one of those folding metal chairs he used for conferences at his desk, and it squeaked as I leaned back, away from his intensity. He was fiddling with a red pen, tapping one end of it against the top sheet of a tower of papers. He was a nice guy, one of the younger teachers who still thought their work was noble. There was chalk dust in his hair.

"She finds it hard to talk to people. Do you?" he asked.

Finally, something I could laugh at. "No! Most of the time I open my mouth and stuff comes out. Too much stuff. That's what my mom would say."

He smiled, but he didn't look convinced. "Anyone would look at you and think there couldn't possibly be anything wrong in your life. But even the most outwardly happy people can struggle with their emotions," he said.

I nodded. Nothing to argue with there.

He shifted in his chair, and I became aware of the loud ticking from the clock above the board. He let silence settle around us.

I was just about to say, *Look, I wrote a story about a character. It was fiction. I'm not about to kill myself!* but then something funny happened. My throat got clogged with tears. "I'm not sad," I managed to say.

"Phoebe, it's okay to be sad. These years can be the hardest years of anyone's life. There's so much going on, and you're trying to figure out how to be an adult in a world that's increasingly confusing."

That made me cry harder. I was so embarrassed, but his face showed nothing but concern and kindness. I wiped my eyes with my fingertips and tried to get control. But more tears seeped out.

"It's just . . . my family's changed. I have a little sister now," I managed to say.

"And there's not much energy or time left over for you," he said.

"I feel so stupid," I said, blowing my nose into the Kleenex he handed me. "Who's jealous of a baby?"

"It's perfectly natural to miss the relationship you once had with your parents."

He seemed like he wanted to listen, so I told him how it used to be when I'd get home from swim practice. Mom would come to meet me at the door and give a huge hug. We'd talk about our respective days while she'd walk me over to the fridge and pour me a big glass of Arrowhead water. I never had the heart to tell her I was already well hydrated and carried my own bottle . . . but it didn't matter, the water Mom poured tasted better anyway.

The way she looked at me just made me feel like she was intensely interested, that whatever I had to tell her was the most fascinating thing she'd heard all day. Her love for me radiated from her eyes.

But now that Tabby was born, sometimes she didn't even acknowledge my coming home. I'd walk through our house to find her. Sometimes she'd greet me with an eye roll, depending on how hard her day had been—not aimed at me, more sort of at Tabby, but it still hurt. Other times, she was laughing her head off at something cute Tabby had done; it felt like an inside joke that they shared, even when she described what it was.

Steven was the same way. He'd arrive home and instantly take Tabby off Mom's hands so she could relax
and start dinner, so any kind of real discussion I tried to
have with him was overrun by her. We'd try to talk over
Tabby's head, but Tabby always interrupted.

"I really love her," I told Mr. Pelkey. "She's such a cool
kid. She's going to be amazing someday. She learns
everything so fast."

"But she's stepping on your toes," he said.

"A little," I admitted. I leaned down to look for his
metal trash can to throw away my wet tissues, and he
nudged it toward me with his foot.

"I'm glad you shared all this with me. I want you to
know I'm here for you anytime. I'm happy to listen. And
I can also get you in touch with some people who can *really* help you if you think you need it."

Silence fell between us again. I knew what he meant.
"I'm not sad like that," I said. "I'm okay."

He nodded. I was just about to stand up, when he
asked, "Can I give you a phone number?"

It was a suicide hotline that he had written on a Post-
it note preprinted with a picture of a German shepherd's
head. *Oh my God. This did not just happen.* My mind reeled.
He actually thought I could do it. He was giving me a
goddamn suicide hotline number. I bowed my head over
it while my face burned. Wow, this was really heavy.
What on earth could I say?

"You must have a dog," I said inanely.

"Yes," he said. "Betty. She's eleven. Getting gray hairs
under her chin."

"That's pretty old in dog years," I said. I stood up. "Thanks for this. I don't need it, though."

"I know," he said. "It's just in case. And you can talk to me anytime. I mean that."

I wondered if I was supposed to hug him. How often do teachers in a big high school like this bother to have such an intense conversation with a student? He truly cared about me, and that showed in every inch of his worried face looking up at me.

Instead of a hug, I lightly touched him on the upper arm. Even that felt weird. "Thanks," I said.

"You bet."

I mustered up the most genuine smile I could under the circumstances, and picked up my books from his desk. I'd have to go to the bathroom first, to make sure my face didn't look like I'd been crying, before heading in to trig. If there had been a quiz, by now it was over.

"I won't read that story to the class," he said. I turned back, surprised.

"It's okay if you do," I said. "It's not a big deal."

I walked back across the classroom, feeling his eyes on my back. He thought it might be the last time he'd see me, before I went home and offed myself.

"Thanks, Mr. Pelkey," I called when I opened the door, but I didn't look back.

I opened my eyes.

I was sitting on the floor of the den. Sheets of paper surrounded me in a fan shape. It was a perfect, deliberate crescent. Cramped handwriting covered every page.

I gave a half scream and scrambled backward, as if the words were insects.

Had I written all this? I didn't even remember managing to pick out a pen, let alone getting the paper.

I crawled back to look at what was surely the first sheet, the one on the far left.

You invite me to write . . . well, I shall, it started.

This wasn't my handwriting. The letters were so tiny they were difficult to read. And . . . it looked like the old-fashioned kind of writing where *s*'s were *f*'s and grandiose flourishes marked each capital letter. While I was sitting here daydreaming, Madame Arnaud had manipulated my body, moving the pen to her own use.

Apparently legend has soaked the countryside about my unholy appetite, she wrote. *Half-toothed quarter-wits kneel by their firesides and tell the tale of Madame Arnaud . . . or perhaps there are no firesides anymore. From the glass tower atop the manor, I rarely see evidence of smoke wending upward on a crisp autumn twilight.*

It had actually happened. She had used my body. There was no way I could've written this myself. I swallowed hard. Had she used my right hand? That was the one I wrote with. I tried to control my shaking, then settled back on my heels and continued reading the entire fusillade of pages.

But regardless, they must be telling the tale . . . they must be, for no one comes. No children—their blood

*heart-stoppingly fragrant—tap upon the door to be let
inside. No workmen come to repair the stones that have
begun to list. My parade of servants, with their starched
aprons and caps: somehow they dwindled while I failed
to pay attention, until one day no one came when I rang
the little golden bell. I yawned in my bed, with its
tapestries wrought by the finest French artisans, and
awaited the tea that never came.*

*I slept again, and then rose, my throat acid with
anger, crusading down the hall to strangle whatever maid
had neglected her service . . . but as I walked I realized
I couldn't remember the maid, couldn't think of her eye
color or the shade of the hair tufts that escaped her cap.
Who was my last lady's maid?*

*And no one was in the kitchens at all; a thick
layering of dust covered the pots and kettles that had
been in hourly use. The gigantic brick hearth contained
a stubble of wood ash, which I bent to and found cold.
Outside, I raced to the stables and there was nary a
horse and nary a stable hand and nary a smithy. The
wooden stalls didn't even smell of horse any longer. All
the smith's tools were scattered by the forge, as if he had
intended to work again and had simply stepped away.*

*I went outside again and stared at the gardens;
nothing grew in order. There was a tangle worthy of
some fairy-tale thicket a prince must work his way
through. The topiary had grown outlandish and lost its
borders; one could no longer detect that these had been
deer, wolves, and rabbits playfully rendered in bush. I
peered through the filthy window of the potting shed*

where previously seedlings had been moved from pot to pot by the diligent gardener, or his son as he grew, or the son's son as he grew, but this time the crockery held nothing but air.

Back inside, I walked room to room. Furniture was missing! An entire estate's worth of vases decorated with hand-painted goose girls; voluptuous ottomans; curved couches that could hold six or seven women, including their ample skirts; rugs that had been knotted by virgins who grew blind for it; the lamps that had cast a gentle glow over all the people who had attended my balls—the nobility who traveled great distances to see Madame Arnaud again—oh, it was all gone! And in their stead, a covering of dust as thick as my own hair spread across a pillow. Although the wing in which I kept my bedroom still retained its furnishings, the rest of the house was bare.

I combed the manor: I was the only living soul there. And I went back to my bed and gazed upon it—how long had I slept? I must have been in a fog, a delirium of that which I drank, because I never noticed the house emptying. How does an entire household vanish while one dozes?

And if they had sold or burned my furnishings, why did they leave my wing intact? Were they frightened to wake me from my strange sleep with the dragging of bureaus and armoires?

I spent an entire day in marvelment. What had happened, and why was I untouched? If they all left me,

knowing what they knew of the doings in my household,
why had they not murdered me while I slept?

Perhaps they had tried.

That night so very long ago, as I went to my bed
fearful I might sleep another century or so, I found a
great surprise as I peeled back the bedclothes. I hadn't
noticed when I arose that morning, but I had slept with
a knife. It was a maid's knife, the kind she tucks into
her apron pocket for opening letters or cutting twine.
Someone had tried to murder me: *feathers poked*
up from holes in the mattress. As enraged as I was at
the thought of a knife plunging between my ribs, I was
equally furious that she had ruined the work of Louis
Des Anges, the premier mattress maker of Versailles.
Hundreds of swans' feathers had been selected for this
particular bed, deveined and washed with rose water
until soft and fragrant as a cloud, then sewn into the
golden ticking that some rat-brained maid had dared to
spoil.

But if she had been stabbing me and not simply the
mattress, why were there not bloodstains? Had the Louis
Des Anges feathers spread their wispy fringes to gather
the blood, as swans may stretch their wings for rain, and
somehow returned it to me?

Why had her treacherous murder attempt failed? My
strength, her weakness?

It hardly mattered since I could no longer recollect her
name or face. I did know that I had to do her work . . .
a noblewoman without any servants.

*So, now, I dress my own hair, pushing away spiders
that nest there overnight and picking out their egg
clusters. I myself choose my gowns from the smear of dry
rot in the closets and cupboards. Some days I fetch my
own tea, bringing it to myself on a lacquered tray foxed
with age; other days I don't bother.*

*I miss being waited on. I miss many things. Fine
things. In France, we drank champagne like it was water.*

*The monk who perfected its aging said it tasted like
stars. So we drank stars, the aristocracy: a bit of the sky
was our due. I shan't forget the sight of hundreds of
glasses carefully filled by servants with the lightest of
amber—so light it was almost clear—frothing from
within like an excitable child.*

*I have always loved a beautiful vessel filled with a
delicious drink. And sometimes what I choose to drink—
dear Phoebe, you shall learn!—makes that champagne of
centuries ago taste of nothing. Rather than stars, I
swallow moons and galaxies and the vastness of space.*

*Back then, children meant nothing to me. I was so
young myself. Then I left the elated pleasure of France
to travel across the water to dark England with the
grudging shuffle of my extended family . . . excepting
of course my despised sister. If France is champagne, this
country is common ale. I'll never forget the brutish wind
on that crossing and the heavy roll of the boat on the
waves.*

*We found land that called to me, that I knew from
stories told to me, in a forest deep enough to provide a
warren for me to wander in my belled skirts. But I*

discovered I took no pleasure in it unless accompanied
by a gaggle of other laughing women. Believe me, my
brother and his wife, and the odd aunts and uncles and
their offspring that constituted our family, were not as
high-spirited as me.

All of us were sobered, dampened, by this brooding
country. The picnics and frolics of Versailles were a long
way from these dim woods. Once the manor was built,
I had a man paint my friends onto the wall in a long
mural: Marie, Sabine, Pierre, Auguste, Gustav, Claire,
and dozens of others I was lonesome for, lolling on a
green lawn resplendent with flowers.

I eventually retreated to the house since walking the
grounds only reminded me of what I had lost. But I
found a sort of happiness. We began hosting balls in our
glorious ballroom. Once again, champagne poured from
the necks of elegant green bottles. I gazed at the gowns
of women who had money enough to care about the
fastening of the bodice, or whether a length of ribbon
had been woven by cheap shopgirls or by devout Irish
nuns handpicked for that purpose by God.

I simply stopped leaving. Outside, the cold sun knew
my abnormal heart and cast cruel light into my clouded
eyes, making me blink like a subterranean beast brought
to the surface. The fine soles of my silk slippers fell prey
to the ravages of pebbles digging into my arches, trying to
insinuate a tear.

The manor was large enough to stretch my legs.
Plus—it loved me. I felt this. It approved of my
furnishings, my draperies. It adored me playing a trick

on a woman who should have recognized it, for it was her own trick! And under my firm tutelage, the estate tempered the forces that had otherwise provided tumult. I will always preside over these stones, healthy and strong . . . years and worlds after Marie, Sabine, and the others laid their elderly necks upon a monstrous device and were beheaded. The manor and I are a perfect couple, in love endlessly.

I've so much more to tell you. I have plans, ideas. You

It just ended there. Mid-sentence.

My mouth was dry, and I felt incredible disquiet radiating through my body. I knew I should feel some sense of relief—I had proof now—but that was the furthest thing from what I felt. Madame Arnaud had plans for me.

She was thinking about me. Plotting about me.

I was somehow her target just as much as Tabby was. What could she possibly want with me? I tried to control my shaking hands, to reach down and pick up the pages. I was going to gather them up in reverse order, so that the first page would be on the top of the pile, ready to hand to Mom and Steven to read. My fingers nearly touched the spidery script . . .

. . . and all of a sudden Miles was there.

I shrieked and stumbled up to stand, nearly stepping on the pages.

"Sorry!" he said, spreading his hands wide like I was about to attack him. He came farther into the room and made a sheepish face. He was wearing black jeans and a close-fitting slate-colored henley shirt with the sleeves pushed up below his elbow.

"What are you—how did you get here?"

"There are lots of ways in," he said. "I hadn't seen you for a while, so I thought I'd come round."

"Did my mom let you in? She knows you're here?"

He shook his head, grinning. My jolting heart began a new rhythm, for a new reason.

"You scared the crap out of me!" I said.

"Sorry," he said again.

I stared at him and realized he was a daredevil, an inch away from being an asshole if he wasn't so handsome. He was here to check up on the Madame Arnaud gossip, slipping in through a window like the mansion belonged to him. Like a common burglar. He'd told me the legend and come to see how much it had scared me.

"Look at these," I said, pointing to the array of papers on the floor.

"What are they?"

"Read them," I said. "Read this one first." I pointed to the one on the left, where the crescent of pages started.

He knelt to read while I studied his face. It was a nice chance to stare without him knowing. From this vantage point, his eyelashes were lush against the sturdy planes of his face. Confirmed: he was still ridiculously handsome.

He frowned. "You wrote this?"

"No. She did."

"Madame Arnaud?" He looked up at me like I was a leper about to wipe my ooze onto him.

I was going to insist "Yes," but I thought about the research I'd done with Bethany all those months ago, the sheet we'd written up with notes about schizophrenia. I paused. What was true?

"I didn't write it," I said. *But Mr. Pelkey would have loved it if you had,* I thought.

"Where did you find them?"

I swallowed, worrying I wouldn't be able to say anything coherent. It took everything I had not to walk out of the room and huddle in my lime green retreat. *He could be a friend,* I told myself. *You need friends.* I took a few calming breaths and explained automatic writing to him.

His eyes narrowed. "You let her take over your body? Weren't you terrified?"

"I didn't even feel it," I said. "But you're not supposed to. You're in a trance."

I felt like an idiot talking about this in Steven's office. We were like two awkward actors in a badly blocked scene: no chairs available to us except the single one in front of Steven's desk. I knelt down so I was at least on the same level with him. His eyes flicked to mine, too close. "I'm not sure," I said.

"About what?"

"About what happened. If it did."

He looked again at the pages. "You couldn't have written this."

"But how can it be real?"

"How can it be real," he repeated. Some dawn of understanding showed in his eyes, and he looked sympathetic.

I was on the verge of telling him I'd screamed in front of my mom while she was putting a Band-Aid on Tabby, and she hadn't reacted. I wanted to tell him about seeing Madame Arnaud in the old part of the house, that she'd turned the doorknob and stalked me step by step. That I thought she had bent over my sister in her crib and maybe even . . . done what he'd said. Drank her blood.

"I get the feeling you're reluctant to trust your senses," he said.

"That—that is true," I said. "That is the most true thing I've heard in a long time."

He smiled at me. "I believe you. And I believe this," he said, gesturing to the pages.

"If she's real," I said, "my sister is in real trouble. She's only two."

"Jesus," breathed Miles, his face growing serious instantly. "You didn't tell me you had a little sister."

"Well, and there's something even worse," I said. I took a deep inhale and plunged in. I had to tell someone—someone who would actually listen. "This morning Tabby had some kind of injury on her arm."

"From what?"

"I think from Madame Arnaud. I was there. I kind of saw it. I saw something. She came into my sister's room and she . . ."

"She what?"

"I don't know. I couldn't watch."

"You mean . . . you think she was . . . ?"

I nodded.

"Did you show it to your parents?"

"My mom's convinced it's from an exposed nail on the crib."

"But you told her what happened?"

I hesitated. "Miles." I wasn't sure I could bring myself to admit that either my mom had purposefully ignored me, or I had experienced a full-blown hallucination. Both options were devastating.

"Yes?"

"My family doesn't seem to listen to me anymore."

A big silence fell.

"They're punishing me for something that happened back in California, before we moved," I said.

"Punishing you by ignoring you?"

It sounded barbaric, and completely unlike Mom and Steven. So, possibly the other thing was true. I swallowed hard, blinking back tears.

"My parents do it, too," he said.

I looked bleakly into his beautiful sapphire eyes, the same color as a ring I'd begged Mom for (unsuccessfully) when I turned sixteen.

"What the hell?" I protested weakly. "How could you do that to your own kid?"

"I thought at first they were just preoccupied. Then I figured out it must be some new parenting technique. They always read books and magazines to figure out how to handle me. I guess I was a little bit of a firecracker when I was younger." He grinned, and the change was like a gift from the gods.

I seized on this explanation, seized on his mood. "Yeah, maybe it *is* some kind of fad," I said. "I remember Mom and Steven going to a lot of group meetings with other parents right before we moved."

"They're ganging up on us," he said. "Maybe we should ignore them back."

I laughed.

"But they probably wouldn't notice," he added. His eyes were so beautiful, crinkling at the edges as he laughed, his upper lip slightly crooked over his fantastic smile. I realized that not only was he very handsome, but that I liked him. In that way.

My breathing became shaky. I wondered if the way I was looking at him had changed, that he could tell what I was feeling. My stomach contracted, and I felt a lurch in my chest. He looked away.

"I have an idea," he said abruptly. "Don't laugh, but we could go to the library. Maybe someone who works there could help us."

I nodded, disappointed at the loss of intensity, but also relieved. "I'll try anything," I said, touching his hand for an instant.

He glanced down at his hand. I've always been a touchy-feely person, but maybe here in England people didn't do that.

"Sorry," I said.

"For what?"

"Nothing." I could feel myself reddening, so I quickly said, "Actually, there's a library here in the mansion." I bit down on my lower lip, which was suddenly deep in my mouth. It hurt.

"All right," he said.

"But I don't know if I can go back there."

"Why not?"

Feeling a sheen of sweat descending from my hairline, I told him everything. The organ, the maid's etched window, Madame Arnaud pursuing me with solemn steps while portions of her skull shone through her ragged, decaying flesh.

"You're not kidding, are you." He said it as a statement, although behind it was a question.

"You don't know me," I said. "But I'm trying to tell the truth. Whatever I understand of it."

Miles held my gaze with an earnestness that made my breath hitch into another cadence. "I believe you," he said.

CHAPTER SIX

Tragedy struck yesterday at the Arnaud property with the delivery of a thousand-pipe organ. Harkwirth & Sons Ltd. of London hired local labor to move the three-ton monstrosity into the newly completed east wing and up the stairs. Grenshire citizen Martin Ellis, 51, collapsed when a bend in the stairs brought too much weight to bear upon his person. Under Madame Arnaud's direction, the remaining nine men continued to battle up the stairs lest the organ slip further. After installing the piece, the men returned to assist Ellis, who suffered internal injuries and spent a painful several hours on the staircase spitting blood into a chamber pot secured by a servant of the household, until he succumbed. The incident highlighted strained relations between the French family, still building their manor, and long-term residents. An inquest into Ellis's death will be conducted.

—*Grenshire Argus*, July 11, 1722

*I*nside the library, Miles walked straight to a large book lying open on a marble podium in the center of the room. I hadn't noticed it the two times I'd been in the library before.

"It's the bragging post," he said. "I'll wager you this is the family history."

I came to join him. I saw by the header that the title was *La Famille Arnaud et Leurs Ancêtres*. He murmured the translation, "The Arnaud family and their ancestors."

We studied the page the book was opened to, an engraving of aristocrats in their ceremonial dress, starched ruffs holding up proud heads and rings adorning slender, tapered fingers. The text, all in French, was elaborately tiny and the font too delicate to read.

I reached out and turned the page for him. Dense text. I turned again, and yet again.

"Wait," I said. I turned back to the previous page, a full-color plate. My vision started to waver and fracture . . . no, goddammit! I wasn't going to faint now!

"That's her?" he asked. He bent to read the inscription beneath the portrait, halfway blocking my vision. "It is," he confirmed, turning to look at me.

I mastered my breath, breathing shallowly. There was absolutely no surprise as I looked into the sinister eyes of the woman dressed in court finery, with profuse silk folds encasing her body, and her hair in an intricate chignon. Her mouth was closed in a gentle smile, but between her lips I could see the glint of her teeth. They were sharp and white, the color of bone. Her eyes appeared clear like a mountain lake fed by alpine runoff, but behind them was pure malevolence. It was the Madame Arnaud I already knew.

"Phoebe, she looks just like you," said Miles. He was still looking at me, his face appalled.

"She doesn't!" I said.

"She looks like you with dark hair in ten years, dressed like a . . . what do you call these people?"

"Oh my God, Miles, stop it! *Please* don't say that."

"It's not completely absurd," he said. "She's your ancestor."

"No," I corrected. "My stepdad's ancestor."

He nodded and looked again at the image. "All right," he said softly.

Together we stumbled through translating the minuscule text on the page but there was little about her other than the fact that she'd left her important standing at the court of Versailles to come to England in the early 1700s. The book made mention of the fact that she'd escaped with her family seventy years before Madame Guillotine wielded her terrible influence. The following pages showed later relatives, including siblings and the nephew born to her brother, and his resulting lineage. Madame Arnaud had had no children of her own.

We reached the end of the book. "Can you show me the hidden room?" Miles asked.

I looked over my shoulder, up at the second story of the library where I'd spent so much time terrorized. But it felt so different today: perhaps because Miles was with me, dispelling the sense of my own vulnerability.

As if he could read my mind, he said, "It's creepy, but I don't get any feeling of her being here watching us."

"I know," I said. "But let's go fast."

I led him upstairs and manipulated the shelf until we entered the cramped chamber where a maid had been housed. "Look at this," I said, pointing out the etched window.

He whistled lowly, shaking his head.

"And here's all her stuff," I said, picking up the apron I'd dropped on the floor when I was here before, and going over to the trunk. He joined me.

"My great-grandmother's trunk had a secret drawer on the back," he said. He tried to pull the trunk away from the wall and gave me a wry smile. "Not strong enough."

But I was easily able to move it forward, and sure

enough, lodged in the pattern of the leather, barely visible, was a small drawer.

Inside: a diary.

"You read it," he said. We both sat on the floor, he with his back against the wall and his long legs stretched out. I sat cross-legged facing him.

With trembling hands, I opened the humble paperbound volume and looked at the lovely, careful handwriting in ink. I read the first page aloud to him. " 'This being the book of Eleanor Darrow, servant in the House of Arnaud, and containing her apprehensions about the Mistress and the goings-on that trouble the estate. I set pen to paper on this fourth day of May in the year 1854 . . .' "

I looked up at Miles. His unsettling eyes were fastened on my face. "Go on," he said.

" '. . . because it falls to me to chronicle the wickedness that pervades every evil stone of this manse. Helplessly, we servants watch as events so sorrowful and despicable take place, so strained we are to the point of wanting to release ourselves of the mortal coil.' "

I began reading silently, scanning. I summarized for Miles. "She writes that Madame Arnaud would drive her carriage through the village, looking carefully out her window. She'd pick a child, and ask the mother to send him or her up to the manor to be her special companion. She'd smile and tell the mother she'd teach her child to play the organ. After the first couple of times she had pulled the trick, no mother believed her. But nonetheless they had to hand that child over, to save the rest of their family. They believed that if they didn't do what she asked, she'd have them killed. So mothers gave up their children, giving a long, lingering kiss, making the sign of the cross with the tears she'd spilled on its forehead, and saying good-bye."

"Damn," breathed Miles.

"The child would go to live with Madame Arnaud," I continued. I skipped an entire page that was illegible from the long-ago spilled tears that made gray rivulets of the ink.

"At first it was wonderful. The child would be fed all kinds of sweets never tasted before, and would be allowed to play the organ. Then Madame Arnaud would hold the child on her lap while she embroidered, and somehow or other, as if accidentally, the needle would slip and puncture the child. Madame Arnaud would gently lift the child's arm, or whatever limb had been cut, to her lips and suck away the blood. Just for a few seconds, that first time. In the beginning, Madame Arnaud was secretive, but as time went on she became very brazen. She would openly suck the child's blood in front of me—I mean, in front of Eleanor."

I looked up. Miles was pale.

I read the next lines, feeling the beginning threads of dizziness unraveling in my mind. "And not just for a few seconds, once the child got used to it. No, she'd take a full suckle like a baby at its mother's breast. She drank her fill."

A page was torn out here. I ran my fingers down the jagged edge of remaining paper. What had this servant torn out? Simply another page that could not be read for the tear-smeared ink?

"Go!" Miles said urgently.

"Let's see . . ." I focused on the next entry, skimming. "Madame Arnaud wanted to live forever, and she believed that drinking blood would prolong her life. She thought especially that baby's blood would do the trick. If she drank the blood of a baby, she got to drink its future, all the decades it was expected to live. She drank the potential of that blood, a life just begun, all the things that child could grow up and do."

I read ahead a few lines and looked over at the window across the room. "Eleanor writes that she'd sit at her window, tormented by not being able to help a child. She'd beg the moon to intervene, the stars to cease their cold shine."

"So she's the one who scratched the words in the window," Miles said.

I nodded. "She must be. And it gets worse," I added, returning to the book. "After the child became accustomed to Madame Arnaud sucking at its cuts, she started using a tool. She had a sort of a straw, made of silver. One of the silversmiths in town made it for her. He had to. He knew the stories about workmen who refused her requests dying in strange accidents, falling down half-built staircases, crushed under ill-supported masonry."

I inhaled sharply at what Eleanor next related, her ink growing darker as if she had pressed down her writing implement in agony. "Later, she used it on his own baby. He designed the straw that killed his own child."

"You can stop," said Miles. "It's enough."

I stopped telling him what I read, but I sat quietly and continued. I couldn't have stopped to save my life. Eleanor Darrow wanted me to know. And I would listen.

One end of the straw was sharp like a scalpel, Eleanor wrote, and Madame Arnaud would pick a large vein in the child's arm and drink from it. That was when you'd start to notice it in the infant's face: very drawn and white. The baby would stop dancing around the huge manor and become listless. Madame Arnaud was drinking all of its energy. Eventually the child would take to bed, lost in a huge four-poster, propped up on pillows, and Madame Arnaud would sit on the edge of the bed and drink and drink and drink, her lips pursed around that silver straw. Her eyes would be bright and sparkling, while the child's eyes started to fade. She'd drink everything that child had. *Everything.*

Eleanor had underlined that last word three times. She left the rest of the page blank as if she couldn't bear to sully it with more of her wretched accounting.

On the next page she continued, with an altered handwriting. Perhaps she had had to pause. I wouldn't let myself consider what tasks she might have been called to do in that interval, what child she might have set kind eyes on . . . and yet not helped.

Madame Arnaud would send word to the family that some accident had happened, Eleanor continued. That the infant had fallen down the grand staircase, or been trampled by a horse. After a while she didn't bother to lie very well. Ten children in a row were said to have been bitten by a rat. Madame Arnaud knew no one believed her, and she didn't care.

"How much more is there?" asked Miles tensely.

I ignored him. If he didn't want to wait, he didn't have to. I belonged to Eleanor Darrow and the spell cast by her haunting words of several centuries ago.

I read on, flipping faster. The last page she had written on—although there were many more blank ones remaining—contained her terrified musings on how old Madame Arnaud was.

"She is alive long past the time any woman should have died, yet she never looks a day older," wrote Eleanor. "The older servants tell me their parents served her, and even a generation hence. The blood is preserving her. Her monstrous design has worked."

The diary ended. But I didn't look up, didn't signal to Miles that I'd stopped reading. I needed the time to mull over what I'd read. So Madame Arnaud wasn't a *ghost.* She was still alive, with her skin peeling like lichen off a stone. So how had the automatic writing worked? Had she actually sat next to me writing those pages?

"She's *real,*" I said. I had seen her twice but until I read these servant's words, I hadn't believed it. This woman had charged others to bring children to her—and she drank their blood. Drank it until they died. She had murdered children and now she wanted Tabby.

"We have to show this to your parents," said Miles.

"Along with the automatic writing pages," I said. "They'll have to believe me now."

He stood up, appearing huge in Eleanor's tiny quarters. Somehow I was reluctant to get up. I sat fingering the battered diary cover.

"What if they don't, though?" I asked.

"One way to find out, isn't there?" he asked. He held out a hand and pulled me up. As soon as I was standing, he let go.

"Damn," he said.

"What?"

"It's happening again. The car—"

It seemed I hadn't even blinked my eyes, no chance for the scene presented in front of me to change, but suddenly I was in a car with Miles. I felt no bodily change, but somehow my limbs had rearranged themselves into sitting, and here I was with the landscape whizzing past. The upholstery was warm against my back, and the light through the windshield was too bright for my eyes.

I made a strangled sound, but he didn't react.

"Miles? Where are we?" I whipped my head around, panicking.

We were driving a thin road with the hedge built up as a tunnel around us. Miles was on my right, strong, tanned fingers clutching the steering wheel.

In profile, he looked tense, his jaw set like he was grinding his teeth.

"What happened?" I asked. "What the hell happened?" I tried to catch my breath. Why was he so calm?

The road widened as we approached a bridge. I peered over—below was a shallow river. I could see rocks on the bottom glinting with an ochre pretense at gold.

"It rises in spring," commented Miles tightly. "Even overflows sometimes."

Oh my God, I was hallucinating again. I was like those people Bethany and I had written our schizophrenia report on. My eyes filled with tears, and I tried to keep that from him. Although . . . was he even there?

On the other side of the bridge, I saw a field of wildflowers, but Miles turned left, toward the woods instead. The flowers lured me with their brilliant scarlets and golden hues. Sirens wafting fragrance to me.

"Go back!" I said. "Those were so pretty."

"No thanks."

I almost insisted, but I was like a leaf being carried by that low river, twirling and snagging on rocks, then freeing myself and floating farther.

He drove until it fell dark. We didn't talk. We kept circling around and driving over the bridge. Now and then, he glanced over at me, but it didn't seem like he wanted to talk. He turned on the radio and I relaxed into his music, closing my eyes.

Eventually I remembered.

I had to get back to the manor to help protect Tabby. I had to show Mom and Steven the automatic writing pages.

"Miles?" I said. "We need to go back." He turned to look at me, his mouth opening to reply, and then—

Then instantly I was *there,* crouched at Tabby's crib, gripping the bars like I was a prisoner. He was gone.

Unreal.

What was happening to me? How could I be in her room when a second ago I was with Miles? I whimpered, watching my sister sleep, innocent and harmless as a baby mouse still blind from birthing. I wasn't in control anymore. My body operated according to someone else's dictates. I was a rat carried from cage to maze by the scientist.

That was a dream, I told myself. *Miles and the car were a dream. I've been here the whole time.*

So . . . had we really been in the library looking at the portrait in the book? And reading Eleanor Darrow's diary?

Of course. That had to be real. I couldn't imagine to that degree of specificity. That part had happened, the library and Eleanor's slow, written recitation of terrible details. The fact that Madame Arnaud was *alive.*

I frantically began to assemble explanations.

I must've fallen asleep in the car, and Miles drove me back to the manor. But what about when I'd spaced out while Madame Arnaud was sitting there writing pages next to me, taunting me?

I'd give anything to be in control again. It wasn't fair.

I let go of Tabby's crib bars and took a seat on the nearby armchair.

Eleanor had said evil was in the very stones of the manor. I pictured the workmen who quarried and stacked those stones returning home after the day's labor. Heavy perspiration turned their shirts a darker color. They must have kissed their wives with delicate embraces so as not to get them sweaty, washed up at a tin bucket and changed their clothes so they could tickle their children and talk about the day. They tipped back a pint of ale, hardly aware that they were building the cage for a monster.

Those men had no idea that when Madame Arnaud unpacked all the trunks of finery from France and began her new empire, she would turn her eye to the sprites of the family, the little elves that made their parents laugh. She'd scoop up the ones who crawled upon the floor before they could toddle to standing and point at things: the cat, the candle, the fireplace, the woman in the mirror with blood staining her teeth.

As soon as it was morning and I heard Steven's shower running, I let out a sob. I could relax my vigilance. Tabby had made it through the night just fine. It was time to go gather up the automatic writing pages from the office where Miles and I had left them and show them to Mom.

I padded down the hallway with its runner of gold shag, and made my way to the den. I entered and instantly saw that the half-moon of pages was missing. No sign of it, and Steven's printer tray and pencil cup looked untouched.

I stood like a statue. I had known all along they would be gone. Madame Arnaud was alive. She didn't need my body to write. She'd written those pages while I daydreamed, and after I'd read them, she'd scooped them up and taken them away. She knew I would use them to convince Mom and Steven to leave Grenshire, taking Tabby with us.

But for some reason she wanted me to read them. She wanted to communicate with me.

All of a sudden, my heart leapt. Maybe Mom or Steven *had* found them—maybe Steven had been in here last night to use his computer and gathered up the pages!

I raced back up the hallway. I peeked in Tabby's room on the way: still asleep. I walked into the master bedroom where, surprisingly, Mom was still dozing, too. Since Steven was in the shower, she'd taken advantage and sprawled over onto his side. She lay there like a starfish stretched to its utmost.

I looked around the room, listening to the water run in the bathroom as Steven showered. He was humming to himself. Their closet door was open and I snapped my head away. I had a bad feeling about that closet.

I didn't see the papers anywhere.

Back in my own room, I searched more. Were the pages here? Had Steven left them while I'd spent the night crouched at Tabby's crib?

No sign of them. I sat down on my bed and let my thoughts swarm.

I sat there, long past when the water stopped, long past when Tabby woke up and Mom rushed down the hallway to her, muttering, "I'm coming, I'm coming" . . . just *long*. A long time.

I didn't understand anything.

★ ★ ★

I had a flash of memory—I'd done something. *Bad.* Whatever it was that made us leave California.

I inhaled quickly.

The sensation was gone.

If I could just access that brief half second of information . . . it was like a déjà vu. Something that some obscure corner of my mind remembered, but not the rest.

"Miles," I said. "I can't remember stuff."

We were at the pool again. My feet touched the bottom, scraping along the ragged surface of the painted concrete. We were both up to our chins, two disembodied heads floating. I wasn't wearing my swim cap, and my hair tugged slightly in the water, unfurling around my neck.

"It's okay," he said. "Just focus on one thing at a time. We've got to get your family out of the manor."

"Madame Arnaud took the pages away," I said.

"We'll show them Eleanor's diary, then."

"Don't you think she would have stolen that, too? Did I put it back in the secret drawer?"

"I don't remember," he admitted.

I swore. We were bungling idiots trying to save my sister. And here we were *swimming*? *Fantastic vigilance,* I told myself. *You're like Lincoln's bodyguard who fell asleep at Ford's Theatre,* a fact I remembered from some long-ago history class.

Miles lifted a dripping hand from the depths to brush some of my wet hair up and away from my cheek.

With a mixture of tenderness and sexiness, his fingers

massaged the back of my neck. My head tipped back, my neck arching.

Wow, I thought. *This is happening?*

He took a step closer. Water lapped against my shoulders from the motion. He opened his lips and I did the same, lifting my chin for him.

The gentle hand on my neck grew firm, pulling me closer. I lifted my arms from the heaviness of the water and wrapped them around him. He lowered his head and kissed me leisurely. Water tickled at my earlobe as I curled my body into his embrace.

His tongue was warm, but his lips were cold from the pool, a combination that made me crazy with arousal. My nipples hardened against his bare chest, with my swimsuit a scant barrier between us. My thighs grazed his. I pressed against him, unable to stop myself. We were so close, skin to skin.

But then he pulled away. I shivered in the cold water without his body heat.

"I shouldn't have done that," he said.

"It's okay," I said stiffly. I wiped water off my forehead and wrung out my hair, anything to not have to look him in the eye.

"I have to go," he said, his voice sounding raw and emotional. "I'm really sorry. I feel awful."

He turned and dove under the surface, and in one long push he was at the edge of the pool. He pulled himself up without looking at me and walked away, water streaming down his swim trunks and large calves.

I stayed in the water feeling stupid. Had anyone seen him kiss me and stalk off afterward? I looked around but no one seemed to pay any attention, everyone still doing their laps and messing around with their kids in the shallow end. No one had seen the newcomer so blatantly humiliated.

What had I done wrong?

CHAPTER SEVEN

Of particular interest to the simple townsfolk who, with widened eyes, ogled the shipload after shipload of arriving treasures, was the Hall of Ancestors, a portrait gallery on the top floor of the west wing. Pictured here are several notable examples, particularly one featuring the mistress of the residence herself, Yolande Arnaud, painted by French royal portraitist Hyacinthe Rigaud.

—From *England: Her Cities, Her Towns, Her Pride,* Vol. XII

*T*hat night, I watched Tabby sleep again. What else could I do?

Periodically she flopped noisily from one side to the other, kicking her feet free of the blanket. Then she'd sigh and drowsily pull it back up. My own eyelids never closed.

Deep shame seethed through me as I stared at the pajama sleeve covering her puncture mark.

Hours later, she woke and Mom spirited her away for breakfast. If not for that marker, I'd have no idea what time of day it was. Without windows to note the sun's progress, I was at a loss. Once again I thought how strange it was that there were windows on only one side of the apartment, that our living quarters nested inside the manor like those stout, wooden, kerchief-wearing Russian dolls, each smaller than the one it fit into.

I walked down the hall. I was going to go back to find Eleanor Darrow's diary, and if it wasn't there, I'd try the automatic writing again—Madame Arnaud's version of it. I'd invite her to write to me again.

But as soon as I walked past the den, I saw them. Pages carefully placed on the rug in a row like color samples.

The sheets were riddled with her slanted, aristocratic handwriting. This time she'd done me the favor of numbering them.

Oh, Phoebe, how droll you are! Madame Arnaud had written.

> *I imagined you would have picked up those other pages to bring them immediately to your parents! Aren't you trying to convince them of my presence? The walls have ears, my dear.*
>
> *But you permitted me to scoop the pages up and take them! You left them there!*
>
> *I reasoned, though, that even should they be presented to your parents, they would think the only sane thing possible: that you yourself wrote them. A short story of sorts. So I leave these here.*
>
> *Is your little mind reeling about things you may have been told about me?*
>
> *About the things I myself revealed to you?*
>
> *You shall be my confidante, you lucky girl. And my heir in every sense of that word. I can share with you,*

if you help me. Share what? Yes . . . that thing. That
small thing we call immortality.

When one is obliged to do something unpleasant, why
not try to enjoy it? I have heard the maids whistling at
their dirty tasks after all. And when provided a dis-
tasteful physick, an invalid will manage a way to
swallow it. I have come to regard my grim elixir with
much glee, for it fortifies me and lengthens my life. I
commissioned a special device to enhance my gratification
and it is a handsome bit of handwrought silverwork.
Who could not help but be pleased when bending to put
one's lips to such a piece?

I stopped reading for a second. She was talking about
the silver straw as if I hadn't heard of it before . . . which
meant she had not been privy to my conversation with
Miles as we read Eleanor Darrow's diary.

When this household was full, it was the easiest thing
to swig all that I needed. Children adore me. As I bent
to suck their life's blood from them, their eyes still
twinkled and I raised their mirth even as they subsided
under the thick, bitter veil that these peasants call
Death. I dandled them to Banbury Cross, I brought that
London Bridge down, and all the seamstresses raced at
the children to shake them up with pins and needles (a
fancy I could easily imitate). We let ashes, ashes bring us
to the floor in giggles, and throughout it all, they found
me merry and joyous.

Children love a beautiful face with a pleasant smile.
What is more wholesomely good than that? Nothing, not
even their own mother's crude grin, set in a homely face.
I bought their trust with the coins of my bright eyes, the
currency of my lovely smile.
Sweet young Tabitha is an eager purchaser.

I stopped, my heart racing. It was one thing to see my own name in that dreadful handwriting, but it was terrifying to have her refer to Tabby. She had earned my sister's trust . . . enough that Tabby permitted her to place the straw into her arm. Tabby didn't scream or cry to wake up Mom; she probably just made a face until it was over. My little defenseless sister, and I was doing nothing to help her.

The pages continued . . .

I do not choose to feast on my own kin, yet taboo is a
luxury best reserved for those who aren't starving. You
can help me.
You have freedom, motion, the ability to leave the
manor and its grounds: you can help me procure
others . . . and therefore save your sister. Perhaps.

Oh my God.

She meant for me to help her get other children.

In return for Tabby's life.

No way, no way, no way, no way, no way, no way, no way, no way.

No goddamn way.

But . . . if it saved Tabby?

She wanted me to . . . to, what? Go into town and snatch a child? Pull a kid into the car and drive off?

I never before considered my own family as a source of blood; never small Louis or his cousins who hooted through these halls until they learned the somberness that our very stones radiate.

You may ask, Phoebe, if any of our family ever wished for some of my secret elixir? No, indeed, they all cringed away from my Ponce de León discovery. They feared me, though I never touched their children. But I offer it to you. You may drink with me, in return for obtaining more appropriate sources.

The village is likely full of expendables, as it used to be. Simply invite one—a very young one—to come visit. It is considered an honor to visit the grandeur of our estate.

Now and again, children come in packs peeking through the windows, their hands pressed against the glass as if they are imprisoned in reverse—they never come alone. They are too old for me to win them over, especially since they are poisoned by what their parents tell them by that possibly obsolescent fireplace, and certainly too many for me to grab. Perhaps if I could determine which is the slowest, learning a lesson from my overgrown topiary wolf, who knows which hen has a lame claw.

The mere thought of it exhausts me. I do live, but not as robustly as I once did. Sleep claims far too many hours of my day. The house puts me to bed and orchestrates my dreams: bird calls, hornets' fury, decayed leaf bones, ghosts.

I call upon you to save me. I need to be coddled, as the servants used to do, plumping a pillow under my head, bringing chilled cloths for my brow. Bringing me . . . well, you know what I ask for. Or would you prefer I take Tabitha?

I left the pages there. It didn't matter. Like she'd said, Mom and Steven would think I'd written it, with my big imagination and my teacher-endorsed creative writing talent.

My head was so dizzy, my gut so filled with spinning nausea, that I stumbled a little on my way out of the room. The evil I faced was so much more powerful than anything I could fight.

I couldn't convince Mom and Steven there was danger here.

I couldn't therefore get Tabby out of danger.

I was going to have to watch Madame Arnaud murder her.

Unless I could offer up someone else's child.

I emerged from the claustrophobia of the manor and dragged in several welcome breaths of untainted air.

But it *was* tainted. The winds on these grounds obeyed Madame Arnaud. They blew when she wanted. I looked to the thick covering of woods, which was keeping Madame Arnaud's secrets for her.

If only we had never come here. We'd still be in California, and the halls of the Arnaud Manor would steadily accrue their layers of dust.

What *had* I done? I watched a few leaves skitter across my shoes. Was it something Bethany and I did? Why did I get in trouble and she didn't?

I tried to cast my mind back to that faraway place, that world where my worst worry was whether the mole in my cleavage could be seen in the shirt I was wearing. Had I maybe . . . partied too hard and screwed up somehow? Blacked out so I didn't remember? I wasn't a big drinker and definitely no drugs—I couldn't run the risk of getting kicked off the swim team—and Bethany was always with me; we kept an eye on each other so we didn't get into trouble with guys. Bethany would've kept anything from happening.

I focused and tried harder, fixing my gaze on the upper roofline of the manor. What were those called: crenellations? ramparts? I used to have a plastic bucket that created those rectangular cutouts in the sand castles I made with it. For a moment, I remembered sitting on the sand at Stinson Beach, a child packing wet sand into the bottom of that bucket, hoping the shape would hold, that the castle walls wouldn't fail and slide like salt settling in a shaker.

Maybe it had something to do with Richard Spees.

I bit my lip and walked away from the manor, feeling it at my back like someone about to tap my shoulder. *Leave me alone,* I thought. *I've had all I can take.*

I could walk into town, leave all this behind. I could

follow that twisting roadway until Miles pulled up to me in his car, grinning and leaning across to open the door for me. Except that he wouldn't. He'd kissed me and then run away like he was horrified.

I kept walking. I noted the ruins of a gate I hadn't seen before, that had once blocked the way to the manor—someone had chipped away at it to reopen the drive, and left a pile of the bricks by the side. Where was one of those hallucinatory episodes, to rescue me? Couldn't my mind zap me to the pool, or send me to the flower field just over the bridge that Miles wouldn't drive to? For once, I wanted to be yanked away; I would gladly give up control. I just wanted to be somewhere, *anywhere* else.

I left the driveway and cut through the trees. I heard a single bird issue a strident whistle. The trees had impressive root systems that gnarled through the dirt like ragged-skin serpents, making it difficult to walk without stepping up and over them.

I came into a small clearing. In the middle, I saw a little stone cottage nestled amid thick foliage. My jaw dropped; Steven had said there weren't any neighbors for miles around.

This was a tall structure, but its facade was meant to emphasize its coziness. It looked a bit like a grotto, with handpicked rocks hewn into place to suit each other. Moss grew over the stones. There was one small wooden entrance, curved like a chapel door, with a brief set of stone steps leading up to it. Ever since I was a child, I had pictured Hansel and Gretel's cottage as something wooden with a thatched roof, but now I was rethinking that.

They might live in a stone cottage such as this, in the very heart of the woods, where inside they baked bread, never dreaming their father would push them into the wild.

I climbed the flight of stairs. I don't know what I was thinking, that I'd just knock on the door and introduce myself? Ask for help fighting Madame Arnaud? I reached out and turned the doorknob, made of a single, perfectly round gray stone.

The door was unlocked.

A wave of strong emotion came over me. My heart started pounding. I left the door slightly ajar and ran down the steps. I sprinted until I felt far enough away from the house to really see it. I turned and looked.

The tiny cottage . . . not so tiny. The huge panel of rock, I could now see, rose several stories. The roof towered far above. I began to suspect something.

I ran around to the side of the house, and what I had feared was true. Behind the charming little facade stretched a *lot* more house. Eons of stone, a quarry's worth. I was just at the head of the snake.

It wasn't just any house. I had stumbled across the entrance to the western wing of the Arnaud Manor.

I inhaled through the sensation of panic; maybe I could push it back. I stood without moving for probably ten minutes, looking at the western wing that had so nearly deceived me.

Climb to the roof, said someone.

It didn't even sound like the voice in my head.

At each corner of this wing's facade, the stones met and

overhung each other, protruding at different lengths to form a sort of staircase to the roof.

Climb.

Then I was doing just that, my hands finding straightforward purchase in the cross-hatched stones. It was unbelievably easy, like someone had devised a false Mount Everest so anyone could climb it. The notches in the stones were large enough that both my feet could rest on them securely before I reached to the next level and pulled myself up.

I stretched my arms overhead—just the perfect distance to have to stretch a little, but not so far that it was difficult—to grasp the stone above me and lever myself up. My body was used to stretching like this. When I swam the freestyle stroke, I always tried to stretch each arm just a bit farther than it wanted to go, to lengthen my stride and increase my speed. The stones were warm against my palms.

Somehow, in the honest effort of climbing, I relaxed.

On the roof, I stood looking in all four directions and saw how amazingly isolated the house was. Despite the fact that cities were booming and populations were out of control in other parts of the world, here Steven's family had a monopoly on miles and miles of land. From this vantage point I couldn't see all of the grounds, but could see the footprint of the manor and a colossal glass tower, like a goblet resting on the roof.

If I squinted, I thought I could almost see the tiny poke of a church spire from the town, but other than that, nothing. Just a field of greenery stretching as far as the eye could see. We were remote here. Like princesses constantly spinning thread in a haunted castle the world had forgotten to tell the knights about.

I walked the top of the roof, wondering how long it would take to reach the main wing. Then I saw the hole.

It was the size of a room, and apparently somebody already knew about it, because they'd put a rusted metal grate over it. I wondered how old the grate was. Had the same people who created the modern apartment laid it down? Or was this older? It looked antique, almost like a medieval dungeon gate laid horizontally rather than vertically.

I got down and crawled on all fours to see better. I was entirely on the grille, suspended in midair. The metal pressed uncomfortably against my hands and knees as gravity weighed me down. I lowered my body fully so I was flat on my belly, my hands now useless if I needed to quickly scramble off the grate.

But the view was worth it. Although the part of the manor Steven had shown me was completely empty, this wing was furnished.

Through the hole in the roof, I could see into a hallway, part of one room, and down the landings of a grand staircase. This was a double-sided staircase and on each landing the two sets of stairs joined for a moment, then split apart again down to the next floor.

I saw brilliant-colored carpeting, the hues of exotic parrots and flora and berries. Monumental, carved bureaus hulked next to delicate, golden couches. There were marble tables, their tops swirled like ink in water, where someone could leave a punch glass, and hooks on the walls for gentlemen's hats. Jade pots stood on the floor, held by cherubim who stretched chubby arms around the bowl's circumference. I saw stuffed peacocks, their preserved, sturdy legs still holding up their bodies and their panoply of feathers. A giant hourglass stood against one wall, its sand completely run, doughy and slanted in its glass prison.

The place was brimming with lavish furnishings, and none of it seemed dusty. In fact, none of it had water damage or rot, which was odd since it lay directly under an open hole in the roof.

All of a sudden, I got the feeling someone was looking at me. I raised my head; I was alone on the roof.

I frowned, and looked down again. Somehow I hadn't previously noticed the portrait gallery. The walls held enormous oil paintings of generations of Arnauds. They were clustered in different rows and layers, a total hodgepodge of paintings that stretched nearly to the ceiling.

I turned my head, and directly beneath and to the left of me, close enough that I could reach through the bars and touch it, was the painting of Madame Arnaud, the same one that was in the book. It was almost like she was there in person, like I had turned a corner without thinking and seen her standing in the middle of the hallway.

I gave my lurching heart a moment to calm. She was crafted of oil paint—she was nothing but canvas stretched into an ornate frame. Someone had made her from pigments and a paintbrush, layering colors to get her skin to emanate that sheen, to get her eyes to flash with a glint of lead. Despite her diamond necklaces and upswept hair, her beautiful face was lined with cruelty, her head at a haughty angle.

The painting's eyes were focused slightly upward, and I was directly in the line of her gaze. Her pupils, which would have been round if she had been staring forward, were half-moons tucking under her upper eyelid. "It's just a picture," I reminded myself. However, I didn't like the coincidence that I crawled out to the spot that was closest to her painting.

The thought arose that if the metal grate were to collapse, I would fall into the manor, the painted eyes drifting down to look at my body huddled on the floor.

Madame Arnaud's eyes focused intently on me. I returned the stare to see if she would blink. I watched her cheeks, the color so carefully planned by the artist to mimic a noblewoman's blush, to see if I saw any sign of breath.

"It's just a painting," I told myself again.

And just to prove it, I crawled closer.

I put my arm down through the grille and touched the frame of the painting. My hand lingered on the rich gold scrolls of the frame, itself a work of art with its carved tumultuous waves. I knew that to be really brave, I would have to touch Madame Arnaud's face.

It'll be okay, I thought. As soon as I felt the thickness of oil paint under my fingers, I would crawl off the grate and climb back down.

I looked again at the painting, at her eyes staring up at me. My hand was trembling, but I forced it to move over toward her face. *It's just a painting,* I told myself.

With a surge of energy, I brought my hand within an inch of her cheek. Madame Arnaud laughed, a breathy, ice-in-glass chime of hilarity.

I screamed and snatched my hand away, scrambling backward on the grate. Her hands came out of the frame and grabbed up through the bars, the large jeweled rings on her fingers clanging against the iron. I stood up once I had reached the roof, still screaming, and began running for the front of the wing, where I had climbed up.

I didn't care if I fell. I flung my leg over the wall and started scrambling down. I scraped my leg against the stone, and felt that dragging spike of pain that meant I'd skinned my knee. I saw the bright blood smear on the stone as I kept propelling myself down. I went so fast I punctured the air—all the molecules roiling and spinning off each other like water in a boiling kettle.

My hands were trembling and my legs just somehow lunged from ledge to ledge. It was almost like I was falling—my body took over from my brain. In disbelief, I felt my feet touch the ground again. Backing up, I leaned down to put pressure on my bleeding knee.

No one was following me.

I looked up toward the roof, expecting to see a flounce of velvet skirts as she began descending. The sky above was gray and mottled, like abandoned oatmeal.

I kept seeing that arm reaching for me, spindly and otherworldly, mobile centuries after it ought to have decayed. What if I had been slower? Would she have pulled me through the grating, like a cat tugging a mouse out from the wall?

Would she sample my blood and do me the twin disservice of insulting its taste with a winched-up face at the same time she murdered me? Would she spit it out like a wine taster but then against her better judgment reach for more?

Sweet Jesus, what I wanted to do was find my mom and howl while clutching her in a world-ending hug, but the same force that made me climb to the roof offered another suggestion.

Walk this way, over here.

No thank you, no thank you. Yet somehow my obedient feet walked not toward my family, but instead to the back side of this wing.

The family cemetery was here, statues and mausoleums gleaming white among the thin black trees.

CHAPTER EIGHT

Bethany and Phoebe,
Great job on your presentation. You provided an in-depth,
sympathetic look at this often-misunderstood disease. I know
the class especially appreciated your photocopied writing
samples from actual patients, as a way of concretely
demonstrating the "garbled thought" aspect. This was an
excellent overview, but you failed to address what happens to
those who go undiagnosed: what danger do they pose to
themselves and others? Grade: A-

—Ms. Avila's grade sheet

I wandered the cemetery, looking at each monument for the name Yolande Arnaud. I wanted to prove that she had died, was deep under the earth. That stolen blood did not permit her to still draw breath into her antiquated lungs other than in troubled teens' hallucinations.

The statues' faces showed they were lost in contemplation, their marble lips just beginning to murmur. Covered with graying moss, they twisted their bodies in various postures of grief, their garments clinging to a stone hip before falling to the monumental feet.

One woman knelt on verdigris knees to lift her iron arms in misery to the skies, her hair streaming behind her as she faced eternity's wind. Another leaned against an enormous urn, draping a graceful arm across it as she mourned, pressing her cheek to its curvature. I saw life-sized weeping willow trees rendered in stone, and a marble book the size of a Saint Bernard, lying open so you could see one "page" had been torn out—the life cut short.

There were also mausoleums—small stone structures that held coffins aboveground. Each had a stained glass door flanked by dull-faced angels, either to prevent the inhabitants from leaving or to prohibit those who would disturb their rest.

While cemetery statues usually express simple grief over death, these seemed agonized. I wondered if the stone-cutters designed them to show how the Arnauds hated what one of their kind did to children. For these marble people represented Arnauds, of course—generations of brothers, sisters, who watched their elderly aunt Madame Arnaud somehow never sicken or die. They suffered the guilt she never felt.

I would jump to the sky in exultation if I could find Madame Arnaud's stone, to prove that she had died just like everyone does, like everyone expected her to.

No luck. Many Arnauds had lived in the house and died, but not one of them was named Yolande. I had worked myself into the last row of monuments at this point, and I rested my hand on the fence that enclosed the rear of the graveyard. The undergrowth flourished here, with weeds pushing their strident hands up to the sky, and I almost expected to see a butterfly wheel out of there, ochre and ethereal.

But in a moment, as the gate opened beneath the weight of my hands, I saw what the lushness was for: cover. It was to hide what I had stumbled upon.

The secret, back part of the cemetery.

I stepped through and stood with my mouth open, helpless. There were hundreds—yes, *hundreds*—of wooden tombstones in distinct rows, stretching far back. They were low to the ground. Child-sized.

Not all of the grave markers had names on them. They didn't need to. Madame Arnaud hadn't cared what a child's name was.

In horror, I read a few names that had been marked: PATRICK AHERN . . . MATILDA SMOLEN . . . FANNY AL-BRIGHT . . . I stopped. It felt too overwhelming.

Underneath each of these tombstones was the dried-out body of a child. Just a kid. Someone, a little boy, whose mother had been too scared to prevent Madame Arnaud from taking him away. A kid who sat at the organ and played a few notes, laughing, and wondered why the beautiful woman got so interested when his finger got a cut and bled, why she insisted on putting his finger in her mouth.

Their lives had been stolen from them. They had never learned what they would look like as adults. Had never seen their parents again. Their last sight, as the final ounce of blood was pulled out through Madame Arnaud's silver straw, was her terrible face, getting redder and redder with *their* blood coursing through her veins.

The mantra resonating through my head was what Eleanor had scratched into glass: *Poor little babes.*

I left the sordid children's cemetery, walking through the hidden gate and past the bleak marble statues of the Arnaud burial ground. I looked at the high back of the house rearing up, and hated its very sight. So much evil had happened here.

Driving with Miles again.

I sat there, watching him make decisions: where to turn right, where to turn left. He didn't acknowledge I was there. He drove faster, though, the more I stared at him. I wanted to reach over and run my fingers down the stubble on his jaw, but I imagined he would pull away. Finally, I couldn't stand it.

"Are we going to talk about what happened?" I asked.

"You mean . . . the kiss?"

"Yeah. The kiss."

He was silent a long time, so long that I turned my head to the window and said, "Never mind. You know what? Just pull over and I'll get out. I can walk home."

"No! I'm sorry, I'm trying to figure out what to say. And it's hard."

"It's not hard. You're not into me. It's fine! No big deal. Just pull over."

"That's not it," he said. "I *am* into you." He paused. *"Quite."*

I sat there, not looking at him. My heart was racing. I waited.

"The problem is, I have a girlfriend."

I blinked. Of course. *Of course* a guy this handsome

wouldn't be free. But then he shouldn't have been kissing me . . . which was exactly what he'd said at the time.

"I keep trying to break up with her," he said.

"Trying?" I rolled my eyes even though I was still looking out the window and he couldn't see me.

"Yeah. Trying. But it's like she's always doing something, or on the way somewhere else. She won't stop and talk to me."

"Sure," I said.

"No, really," he said. "It's not an excuse. I want to break it off, but I don't want to just shout it out to her. I want to sit down and do it nicely."

Somewhat grudgingly, I nodded. I managed to turn my head and look at him. He took his eyes off the road for a second to give me an apologetic smile.

"So that's where I'm at. I'm not free, but I will be soon."

"Well, let me know when you manage it," I said.

"I will," he promised.

I sucked in a heady amount of air at how the expression on his face made me feel when he glanced over again. I trembled while his eyes remained locked on mine.

"Oh my God, look at the road," I said. "I don't want to crash!"

He gave a funny smile and looked away. I felt cold without the heat of his gaze and regretted saying anything.

"It's cool that you're being faithful to her until you can break it off," I admitted.

"I try my best not to be an asshole," he said. We both cracked up. His laugh was warm and low and made me want to say brilliantly witty things for the rest of my life to get him to make that sound.

"It's a true burden in life, isn't it? Not being an asshole?"

"It's like . . . so . . . *hard,*" he said.

"I'm working on downgrading myself from bitch to witch."

He laughed. "Never. No one could ever use those words for you."

"You haven't seen me in action," I said.

"I've seen you."

My stomach flip-flopped at that one. Okay, so this was not so bad. He liked me. He even liked me "quite," in all the wonderful Britishness of that word. Soon I'd be kissing him for all I was worth, burrowing my fingers into that beautiful, black hair. I'd take my time and lick a slow trail down his neck into the hollow near his clavicle.

I took a few deep breaths to calm down a little. I tucked my hair behind my ears and faced front again.

Soon we approached the bridge, the one he always turned left after. "Hey, turn right," I said. "I want to see those wildflowers over there."

"Next time," he said.

How many times had we driven this same stretch? I wasn't seeing much of England, but I had memorized every curve and pitch of this road. I rolled down the window and inhaled the dulled air . . . there was a pungency to the atmosphere back home that I missed. The sharp smell of eucalyptus . . . something indefinable in the ocean–meets–city aroma. California.

California. My family. My *sister*.

"Oh my God," I said. "Madame Arnaud left me more pages. She wants me to . . . she wants . . . Miles, we have to get back."

His jaw dropped as he whipped his head around to look at me.

"We keep forgetting," he said.

I clapped my hands to either side of my face. Why the *hell* did I even care about kissing this guy, when my sister was in danger? "Drive back right now," I said. "I'm such a jerk. If anything happens to her . . ."

He did a U-turn, scraping the car against the brambles that lined the narrow roadway.

And then: we were there. But not where I wanted.

Frustrated, I hit my palm against my thigh. We were standing in the Arnaud cemetery, his car nowhere to be seen. "Dammit!" I shouted. "I want to be inside. Did we walk here?"

Miles shook his head.

"I'm so tired of this!" I yelled. "Who is doing this to us?"

"It's all right," he said. "We'll go inside. Stay cool."

"I can't," I sobbed miserably. "It's my sister. It's my freaking sister and I can't even get my act together enough to help her."

"It's not your fault," he said. "It's just . . ."

"What?"

"Just how the world is operating, isn't it?"

I stared at him, and my panic left as quickly as it had arisen. "No," I said. "This is not how the world works. There's something *wrong*. There's something pushing me and pulling me, and I don't have any control."

He nodded, although his face remained confused. "I don't know why," he said. "But I'll help you with your sister. We're close at least. Let's find our way back into the manor."

I started toward the main cemetery gate, but he didn't come with me. "A shortcut?" he asked. His hand was on the ivy-covered gate.

"You don't want to go in there," I started to say. But I stopped myself. He needed to know.

He stepped through, and I watched his face as his mind was blown. His cheekbones, already so prominent, went into high relief as his jaw slackened in disbelief. His eyes, normally heavy lidded and sensual, went wide as a child's.

I hated the perfect spacing between the rows of small wooden markers, because it looked like someone had been methodical about planning them. Weeds grew as tall as the markers, but there was no hiding the atrocious symmetry of the area. It was darker back here, thanks to the secretive vining Madame Arnaud or her servants had planted. It felt poisonous, as if some of the dark, fertile plant life might rub against one's cheek and leave a residue of venom.

"Maybe this is just some kind of hoax?" I asked quietly. "Anyone can throw up a bunch of wooden grave markers."

He shook his head. "No, Phoebe. Don't you feel it?"

"What do you mean?"

"Just listen to your body. The way you do when you swim."

Listen to my body? When I swam, I *forgot* my body. I was nothing but breath. But I tried to do what he said. I stared off into the distance, where the ivy clung to the walls of the manor. And I allowed myself to turn up the volume on my strange, whistling undercurrent of knowledge.

I heard sadness, aching generations of sadness, with one bright crimson stripe of brutality, like chamber music with a single electric guitar banging out dissonance. Or a chorus of monks chanting, while a deranged soprano threaded her screech through their piety.

Some say the past is like a groove in an old-time LP record. If the needle skips, you hear it again. But somehow Madame Arnaud's legacy had embedded itself into every channel of that wax, softly behind the regular track.

"I feel it," I said.

He reached out his arms and hugged me. His shaved jaw lightly scratched my temple.

"I'll help you," he whispered into my ear. His voice had the deep rumble of someone far older, a man who'd smoked cigars all his life. I could sink into that voice, let it comfort me through nightmares, through all the nights I might sit up unable to sleep.

"Thank you," I said. I told him what I knew I had to

tell someone. "She wants me to bring her a child from the village."

"Are you serious? How do you know that?" His eyes searched my face.

"She wrote me more pages. She said she'd let Tabby go if I could bring her someone else. It's taboo for her to drink her own family's blood, but she's starving."

He hugged me again, and I closed my eyes to inhale his particular fragrance of soap and cologne. He stepped back firmly, clearly reminded again of his girlfriend. "I don't know what to say," he said. "But you won't have to secure a child for her if we get Tabby out of here."

He pointed at the thicket of ivy—somehow he had seen a gate handle in the profusion. It was another way out of the secret cemetery, and we found ourselves in the manor's true backyard—the area stretching behind the main wing. Miles stopped short at the sight. I realized I was standing there with my mouth wide open like those antique portraits of Christmas carolers.

This had once been a showcase of a garden—gardens, really—with lawns stretching gently downhill miles into the distance. There were pools with fountains in them, overcome with mold, and paving stones laid in curling, graceful pathways, and trees marking the *grande allée*. White statues, stationed periodically, held graceful poses. Farther off, a long, substantial canal held water.

"It's modeled on Versailles," said Miles. "My parents took me last year. Madame Arnaud must've been trying to re-create it, with her own stamp."

We went down the somewhat-broken stairs to reach

the lower terrace. I looked out into the distance—and my heart jolted.

"What's that?" I asked him, pointing to the small shape emerging from what looked to be a maze. Soon the shape was running; it was human. A toddler.

"What's he doing out here?" Miles asked.

I felt the contradiction of wanting to protect an untended infant and feeling pure terror that something wasn't right with it, that it was part of Madame Arnaud's menagerie.

"I wouldn't call it 'he,' " I said.

It ran toward us in the clumsy way of young children. It had a young rooster's fluff of black hair and still wore yesteryear's blowsy boy's tunic. When it was about forty yards away, it tumbled, and I gasped. It quickly rolled over and stood up again. Running straight toward us.

"Uh . . ." I said. I had no idea what I feared: the toddler's teeth, the unearthly howl that might emerge from its soft, milk-fed throat?

As it got closer, I saw the look on its face. *Not good.*

"Yeah, time to go," Miles said.

We bolted. I kept turning my head to see the fervent progress of the pale, nearly translucent, child. I had seen the infrastructure under its face, the network of tired, emptied veins, the panels of bone and muscle . . . and the desperate wanting that was in its eyes. It wanted something from us.

As soon as we turned the corner to start down the adjoining wing, we slowed to a jog. There was no way the infant could pursue and catch us on its tiny, untried legs.

"What the hell *was* that?" asked Miles.

"You tell me."

We collapsed onto a stone bench covered with the circuitous scrollwork snails had left behind.

"It was one of them," I said. "One of Madame Arnaud's victims."

"So he's not at rest."

"Clearly!" I said. "The weird thing is, there were hundreds of tombstones for the kids. Why isn't this place crawling with ghosts?"

He didn't answer, and I heard my sentence linger in the air. "Am I really talking about ghosts?" I asked. "This is seriously what we're talking about?"

I remembered when he'd first told me about Madame Arnaud and I'd been so skeptical. I felt myself blushing—but it wasn't actually embarrassment, but something bigger, something tinged with queasiness and maybe even anger.

Miles narrowed his eyes at me. "Maybe there are ghosts here, but we can't see them. So why would that boy be any different?"

I released the breath I didn't know I was holding. Yes, we were seriously talking about ghosts.

"I wonder how long the poor kid has waited for someone to come talk to him," I said.

"Poor kid? It looked like it wanted to kill us."

"Maybe that's just because we're not used to seeing desperation so severe. Think about it. Based on his clothing style, he must have been haunting the backyard for hundreds of years."

"You think he just wanted to talk to us?" Miles asked.

I didn't know how to answer. I watched the corner of the manor, wondering if we'd see the scrap of a child stagger around it, exhausted, but doggedly trying to catch up to us. And what would he say? Could he even talk yet?

"Let's keep going," Miles said. We stood up and turned our backs to the possibility of interacting with the boy. We had another child to tend to: my sister.

Sitting glued to Tabby's side, I reflected that another day had passed without my showing proof to Mom and Steven. The pages in the den were gone: big surprise. And somehow we'd been deterred from returning to Eleanor's chamber to get her diary, which would explain everything. Now it was nighttime and I was back on vigilance duty, watching my sister sleeping cluelessly in her crib.

I was supposed to find a substitute, to keep Madame Arnaud from preying on Tabby. I could get Miles to take me in his car. I could look for the worst child, the bully at the school, the bastard who tortured animals. We could research it, find out which child was expendable. And then I'd . . .

Jesus. I couldn't even imagine it. Coaxing a child into the car for . . . my stomach lurched. I just wasn't capable of it, even if it would save my sister's life.

All it would do was buy Tabby time. Because undoubtedly, once Madame Arnaud was hungry again, she'd threaten Tabby again. And I'd have to find another child. I'd be stuck in the pattern until Tabby was too old for Madame Arnaud to want her. *Years* would go by.

I couldn't do it.

How many people, given the chance to save the life of a family member, would do whatever possible? They wouldn't even question it. They would just do it.

I'd never been more dangerous to the world than I was right now. I was walking on the thin crust of a lake covered in desultory ice. Below me, I could see the water rising up, ready to spring, willing to let that ice crack. The water wanted to welcome me into its cold and bracing arms.

On her grade sheet, our psych teacher had said Bethany and I never talked about what happens to undiagnosed patients. What danger they pose to themselves and others.

If this was all an out-of-control delusion, with an illusory Miles confirming it for me, what horrible deeds might I do, thinking I was doing the right thing?

We had moved here to England because I did something wrong, after all.

I'm a good person, I told myself. *I might have made a mistake. But I'm a good person.*

I pulled my mind out of the morass of circular thinking and focused on the little girl in the room with me. I could guard my sister; I could watch her intensely. Now that I knew Madame Arnaud was alive, I realized she was someone I could actually fight. As long as I didn't faint, that is.

All I could do was hover over Tabby so closely I was

able to memorize every inch of her skin. I'd never noticed that one mole over by her ear, nor ever peered in that ear to see the tiny passageway with its slightly yellow walls. I counted her teeth and looked at the pale blue veins visible through the part in her scant hair.

Tabby woke from a nightmare, fussing, and Mom came back in for another lullaby. I felt like a voyeur during the tenderness of her song—the same one she'd sung to me basically until third grade. I know, embarrassing it went on so long, but honestly nothing else relaxed me so much as hearing that one brief song in my mom's light soprano voice.

But as her voice cracked over the phrase "and keep you safe, sweet child, till morn," I fled. I ran back to my lime green room. Then I got confused.

I forgot. I forgot danger, forgot everything. I sat on my bed and I can't say where my mind went or what I was thinking. I bathed in nothingness. I couldn't connect my body and my mind . . . almost like swimming with gravity releasing its hold . . . but in a completely disorienting way that left me devoid of emotion.

I think that then I knew. But I pushed the thought away. Instead, I drifted, taking solace in the vacuum of sensation.

CHAPTER NINE

Born: a son Louis Arnaud, April 14, 1722, to Isabelle and
Henri Arnaud. Henri along with several relatives moved here
from France last year, and a manor house has been built for
them on Auldkirk Lane.

—*Grenshire Argus* birth announcement

*T*he breakfast table.

I was sitting looking at Tabby's toast. It didn't interest me in the slightest. I had no hunger.

"Today's going to be one of the sad days," Mom said. Steven froze with his coffee mug halfway to his lips. He set it down, stood up, and walked behind her chair, leaning over so his cheek rested on top of her head.

Something was so intimate, so private about them that I turned my face away.

"They're all sad," he murmured.

"But today . . . it's debilitating. I can't watch Tabby. I just want to . . ."

"You can stay in bed all day," promised Steven. "I'll watch her."

She reached up a hand and he held it, his thumb caressing back and forth. Mom gave a guttural moan and her mouth shaped into a soundless rectangle—an expression I've never seen before on her face. It was like she was somewhere far beyond sadness, that mere sobbing was not enough to express her profound grief.

But when it did come, her sob was so catastrophic that I cried aloud myself in horror. What on earth had happened to Mom?

Steven was crying, too, quiet tears running down his face and into her hair.

"I'm sorry, I'm sorry, I'm sorry," I said. It was me. I did something. I buried my face in my hands.

"It's not your fault," said Steven. "You have to let go of that."

"It *is*," I said, muffled by my palms. I'd screwed up royally.

I couldn't handle seeing Mom so overcome; it just killed me. And Steven crying, too? That never happened.

I felt so sick the bile rose in my throat. This was the kind of pain nothing would ever heal, like a knife was in my chest, puncturing my lungs, making me fight for every breath past its heavy silver heft.

Misery settled into every cell of my body . . . nestling in with guilt. Together they rode my electrons and protons, terrible masters digging in the spurs.

I'd done something wrong.

What was it, though?

Looking at my mother's tortured face, I'd had enough. I had to figure this out, and *now*. I pushed past all the signals that told me to stop, that it was too hurtful to think about.

I had to know. I had to *know*.

Left arm, right arm, cleaving through the water with succinct splashes. Turn my head and breathe. Legs strong. Hips gently canting. All my bodily systems working in tandem.

Pushing with everything I had, my lungs on fire. *I can relax when it's over,* I was telling myself. *Push through the pain. Pain is temporary, but a win is forever.*

The swim meet against Berkeley High.

I remember this, I marveled. Their lead girl had posted better times earlier in the season, but I knew I could beat her. *Every tenth of a second counts,* I was coaching myself. *Stretch those arms farther, grab as much pool as you can. Quick economical inhales every eighth stroke.* My lungs were burning. Every muscle was burning.

Then . . . the stars. The dizzy constellations behind my eyelids. There they were in all their bright and terrible splendor, a whole skyful taking over my vision. Too many to count, too many to comprehend.

Almost there, I told myself. *Fight it off.*

Couldn't remember if I was close to the wall or not, praying for my fingers to touch the reassuring solidity of tiles. But all I felt was more water.

I was laid out, exposed and helpless, to the starred universe inside myself.

A mouthful of water.

I sank without a fight.

The water won, but I hadn't even tried. Instead, I had

been stargazing, watching the cosmos in the loneliest of nights.

I couldn't bear to attend the autopsy, but I did hover in and listen later when the coroner told Mom and Steven it was long QT syndrome. My fainting spells had been real, were caused by a genetic mutation.

"If she hadn't fainted in the pool, it still would have been fatal," he told them. "It slows the heart."

Since there was water in my lungs, the true cause of my death was drowning, and that's what he told them he'd put on the death certificate. He meant it to be reassuring that I would've died anyway.

As I drifted away to process the news in private, like an animal buries itself in leaves to brood over an injury, I heard my mom ask, "If we'd sought medical advice and gotten her diagnosed . . ."

She couldn't continue, breaking down in tears. Steven finished the sentence for her. "If she'd been diagnosed, could she have lived?"

The coroner said very gently, "You'll need to talk to your doctor about that. This is a very rare syndrome and it would take an outside-the-box thinker to arrive at this diagnosis." He paused for a long time. "But there are medications she could have taken to control the—"

She didn't let him finish. She screamed. She screamed one long, singular sound until every iota of breath had left her lungs.

Her lungs empty.

Mine full.

CHAPTER TEN

The mood was high and the music brilliant at the recent fête held at the Arnaud property in northern England. For many attendees it was quite a drive into the wild. However, the gasps upon arrival into the main hall made it clear that swaying in a carriage for hours on end was certainly worthwhile. Lanterns decorated the lavish grounds while flowers and rich adornments were found in every inch of the interior, a massive and luxurious manor decorated in the Continental style. After the bustle of a busy Season, it was a pleasure to stop at the Arnaud estate for one last hurrah before returning home.

—From the *London Social Whisper*, August 14, 1801

I had a job to do.

I needed Miles's help.

My sweet friend Miles. I understood exactly now. I saw it all. I couldn't believe it had taken me so long to understand. I had to help him understand, too.

But where was he? Every time I'd ever seen him, something threw us together. I had no idea what that force was or how to harness it. How would I find him again? Every time I witlessly landed in his car's passenger seat, or joined him in the fast lane of the pool, I'd had nothing to do with it. It had just happened.

Well, if there's nowhere else to look, try inside yourself, I thought.

Maybe I could call him to me by the sheer fervor of my desire to see him.

I closed my eyes and called to him in my mind.

"Miles, I need you, I need you. Please . . . come."

I felt a stirring in the air surrounding me.

"Phoebe," he said. I opened my eyes and he was there. We were in my lime bedroom. "Are you okay?" His voice held so much tenderness.

"I'm okay," I said. I paused. "I'm working on 'okay,' actually."

He smiled at me uncertainly.

"Miles. Tell me what's on the other side of the bridge," I said.

He looked at me, confused. "What bridge?"

"The one we always drive over," I said. "You never want to turn right."

He nodded, then shrugged. "There's nothing on the other side."

"I think there is," I said quietly. "What would we find if we turned the other direction?"

We were in the car now. The motor sounded scratchy, small.

"I've been trying to turn right," he said in a tight voice.

"Since when?"

"Since I met you."

Whoa. I raised my eyebrows and took a closer look at him, hunched over the steering wheel, seemingly in agony.

"Yeah," he said. "I've been trying to take that goddamn, bleeding turn since I met you!" He thumped his palm on the steering wheel. We were on the bridge now, the water sparkling beneath us like tinsel.

"Here it is, just slow down, just . . . Miles, you missed it!"

He had turned left. I looked at my hands, folded in my lap. This was so cruel of me.

"Do it over!" I insisted.

We were back on the bridge.

He decelerated, and actually began to turn the wheel to the right. But then he stopped the car completely.

"What is wrong with me?" he asked. I pointed to the right, where the field of flowers invitingly wafted in the wind.

"Turn right!" I said. I was firm. My eyes filled with tears, though, the minute he looked away.

The car began moving again. I put my hand out to help steer, but underneath my palm the steering wheel was already moving to the right. He was doing it.

The field was filled to tumult with towering foxglove and primrose. These flowers had caught the chance of a breeze that spread their seed, or bees that had made quick work of delivering pollen. Nothing was planned about this riotous spread of color, with oxeye daisies and pansies and wildflowers whose names I didn't know.

I noticed a huge ditch between the road and the field, somewhat hidden by the way the land fell. I was reflecting that in the U.S. there'd be guardrails here and you'd have to sign a form swearing you wouldn't litigate before they'd let you drive it.

I was about to turn and say this to Miles when he made

a horrible sound, halfway between a sob and a scream. The look of horror on his face would have brought me to my knees if I'd been standing.

He must've taken his foot off the gas, because the car dramatically slowed. He lifted his hands off the wheel and pressed them to his face. The road was fairly straight, and the car drifted lightly to the edge of the ditch before coming, completely undriven and unoperated, to a stop. The heavy air, drooping with pollen, flooded through my open window.

Behind his hands, he was . . . I don't know . . . hyperventilating or crying in some strange hitch-of-his-breath way.

I tried to pry his hands from his face. "Miles, tell me," I said. "I want to hear. I want to know how it happened."

I don't know how long we sat there with me pleading for him to tell me. It could've been hours. The wind picked up and the steady droning sound of the bees working their way through the field ceased.

Twilight eased its way across my vision and I hovered with Miles in the flower-besotted darkness. Hovered, like an insect above the tassel of the bloom, ready to risk everything for just a bit of sweetness.

"I'm so sorry," I murmured.

I pulled away and looked. Broad daylight again, sunlight dappling the foxglove and making a blaze of his windshield.

"You, too?" he asked.

I nodded. I reached out and ran a lingering hand down

his jawline. He was so strong. I could tell he saw things differently now. Like I did. I saw the deadness in him.

"Car accident right here. The ditch isn't that bad, except for that rock." He pointed it out. Then he pointed at his head.

I caressed his thick, dark hair. It had been covered in blood that day, and his skull had been a complex medley of pieces, but now he was handsome and whole again.

"Now I get it," he said. "How everyone's been treating me. Or not treating me, I guess I should say."

"I know," I said. "I kept finding ways to explain it, but it was so awful to be ignored like that."

"What . . ." He snorted, and gave me an apologetic smile. "There's no easy way to say this. What happened to you?"

"I had a rare syndrome that made me faint. I lost consciousness during a swim meet and drowned. All along, I thought I had done something bad, something that made us move here." I paused. "I guess I did. I died."

We sat there for a long time. Or maybe it was a short time, in the grand scheme of things.

"Gillian was with me when it happened," he said. "She wasn't hurt badly. But that's why I haven't been able to break it off with her. She doesn't listen . . ."

". . . because she can't," I said.

"Right. And I could've proceeded anyway, except she was the one who was there. She held my hand when I died. Even though I couldn't bring myself to remember,

I still felt some sense of gratefulness to her for that. And . . . well, guilt for putting her through it."

I felt no jealousy. If death was a wide field of lonesome blankness, I couldn't begrudge him anything he felt for her. He leaned over and arranged my hair for me, tucking it behind my shoulders to fall free. He was inexpressibly tender, his eyes intent on mine the whole time. His fingertips barely touched my skin. I could hardly breathe.

The emotions were so intense that I buried my face in his neck. I took a few deep breaths against the warmth of his throat, feeling his chest pressed against mine, and then lifted my head.

"Is everyone like us?" I asked.

"I don't know," he said.

I remembered a poem I'd studied last year in English class. It was by Emily Dickinson, and about someone who was riding around in a carriage not realizing they were dead. Kind of like Miles in his car. *Exactly* like it, actually.

The poem ends:

Since then 'tis centuries; but each
Feels shorter than the day
I first surmised the horses' heads
Were toward eternity.

I got it now. The eternity. It happened to me on a moment-by-moment basis.

I was never going to be real, ever again. I was a ghost,

a shadow. Someone who could reach through the living only with ineffective fingers. Someone who would talk to loved ones and never get an answer.

"We can worry about our own . . . status . . . later," I said. "I still need to deal with Madame Arnaud. I know for sure she's real now. I'm not crazy, just . . ." My voice trailed off.

"I can understand why you thought you were crazy," said Miles.

His hand was warm, to me anyway. I rubbed my fingers over the bones of his knuckles. He lifted our joined hands to hold my jaw and give me one sweet, quiet kiss.

I could have cried.

I straightened up. "We've got to get back to the manor," I said. "My mom's already lost one daughter. I can't let her lose the other."

But still we sat.

We drifted in our heads as a beehive was crafted, cell by cell, against the underside of Miles's rock, then decayed after generations of bees left for some more wholesome environment.

"You're right," said Miles with a new edge of decisiveness. He turned the key in the ignition. I was amazed at his aliveness. "And who knows, maybe saving your sister is the thing we need to do to graduate, as it were. On to the next realm."

I sat up straighter, reveling in how good it felt to again have a desire, a wish, something to do with myself other than ponder the sad and static fact of my own death.

I could be useful. I could help from where I was. The big sister reaching out a vaporous hand to help her infant sister.

"Let's go," I said.

CHAPTER ELEVEN

Daily functioning at the manor appears to have stopped abruptly sometime in the mid–1850s, as the town tax records show no income from servant wages starting in July 1856. A study of the *Grenshire Argus* microfilms from this period indicate no untoward or calamitous event to explain the shift.

—From Trudy Bilkington's sociology senior thesis, 2008, University of York

We forced ourselves to return to the manor.

It was insane.

A madhouse. Bedlam. So much commotion I hadn't been aware of before.

"What *is* all this?" asked Miles.

Each of the hundreds of windows glowed. The large bay windows outlined in lead, the tiny windows that lit the cramped back stairways servants traveled, the full-moon-shaped windows that made a heads-up coin out of the person who looked out them . . . all lit. The attic windows with gables above them, the gallery of windows that turned a hallway into an ocean liner, even probably the window Eleanor Darrow had scratched her agonized message into . . . all blazed through the darkness.

Through each window we could see frenetic motion, servants dashing from room to room, opening curtains, closing them. The darkening grounds were busy, too, with men carrying bundles from unseen carriages into the house, and the gardeners hoeing, pruning, planting. Everywhere children of all ages nipped at their heels, racing in circles, laughing . . . or solemnly stared out the windows at us, disturbed.

Wanting to make sure Tabby was all right, I motioned for Miles to follow me into the modern apartment. Upon entering, I quickly realized it hadn't always been modern, for there were servants and children here, too. We watched incredible activity: children running. Jumping off furniture. Girls in their petticoats, spinning in a circle to hear the fabric swish against their hips. Boys in their short pants and sturdy leather shoes. They played marbles, rolling the gaseous atmospheres of glass planets across the floor. They played statues, trying and failing to remain motionless.

They bounced a red ball back and forth, in the timeless pattern of childhood, the dull thud of the bounce produced for centuries. Pretended to waltz, half graceful, half clumsy, curling their hands around their partner, the air. Chased each other, dove under furniture, charming, oblivious. And all of them, despite their feverish activity, despite all the noise they could generate—all of them paper-thin and not quite there.

I couldn't pretend that I didn't realize that every single one of those children had been as precious to their family as Tabby was to mine. I looked at Miles sadly and bit my lip.

Adding to the teeming noise, servants stepped around the children, muttering to themselves.

"Ahhh," one moaned as she bustled past me with a pail full of coal. "We should tell, we should get help."

"We never lifted a finger," said another, who was carrying folded linens so high they nearly blocked her face. "We are damned for all eternity. The children!"

"The children!"

Every voice was whispering about the infants of the household, and with a clench of fear in my stomach, I understood why. The servants saw what was happening with Madame Arnaud, but were powerless to stop her. Guilty, shamed ghosts. Damned for all time.

They wrung their rotten hands, they hid their faces in their aprons. They bumped into each other in a haze of distress, wailing their repetitive wails.

The dire chorus was horrible, and we walked past them through the living room and down the hallway. As we passed the kitchen, I saw something extraordinary. Something . . . perfect.

My mom.

It was fairly quiet in there; in Madame Arnaud's day it must've been a chamber few had access to, the original kitchen being located down a level. Compared to the odd children who flickered through, casting amazed glances at the grandeur they still saw, Mom was a beacon of solidity. Her skin glowed with warmth, vitality . . . next to her, the others looked like sheets coming out of a printer whose ink cartridge was running out.

As she washed dishes in the sink, lightly humming to herself, she was so majestically beautiful I could have wept. Her gentle eyes focused on her task, and her graceful fingers moved the sponge around the lip of glasses and into their depths, carefully settling the glasses into the rinse water on the other side.

With my new knowledge, my mom was riveting, a show I could watch forever. I grabbed at Miles's hand: Could he see how spellbinding she was? He squeezed back, but I didn't bother to look at him. My eyes were all for her.

She worked on a pot next, scrubbing so hard the muscles in her forearm flexed. She was strong, she was good.

She was the person I loved more than anyone else on earth.

It had taken death for me to realize that.

I loved Steven and my real dad, and I loved Tabby. Bethany was my closest friend. But in the midst of all my teenaged angst and my rejection of Mom as someone who didn't "get" me, she was always the one I loved the most.

And now she'd never look me in the eye again.

This hit me almost harder than knowing I was dead.

Mom had cheered me on for everything I'd ever done. I could remember her sitting on the floor helping me build towers with wooden blocks, laughing her head off when I pushed them over. She took me to playgrounds and hovered nearby, making sure I was safe as I climbed the structures and hurtled down slides. As I got older, she would hug me from behind as I sat at the kitchen table doing my homework, just a silent, wordless way of her saying she loved me.

They say memory is a collage some artist of the cerebrum creates. I was experiencing it now, brief glimpses of her scolding me; of her pretending to collapse in the snow from some lame snowball I'd thrown; of her letting me use lipstick for the first time, watching in the mirror with an amused grin.

She was holding out a broom for me to sweep up the shards of something I'd broken; she was dancing to a CD of Busy Dick I'd brought home, her eyes widening with shock at the lyrics; she was on the sofa, sick herself for once, while I brought her ginger ale and crackers.

She was angry, she was sad, she was euphoric—and through it all, her eyes glowed with love for me. She loved me so much, her eyes had developed particular wrinkles from the smiles she'd given me ever since I was a baby.

I stepped closer, releasing Miles's hand, and stood next to her at the sink. I couldn't tell what she was humming. I sank sideways, waiting for her solid warmth to support me, to prop me up. But I nearly fell.

"We should look for Tabby," Miles reminded me.

I stared at Mom's profile, her mind busy. What was she thinking about? She had found some comfort doing this mundane task. Her mind was not on me. This was one of the rare moments she had discovered, in which she was free of sadness.

Those moments would be occurring more frequently as the months and years went by.

"Mom, don't forget me!" I cried, and she reacted not a stitch.

"Phoebe, don't," said Miles softly.

Mom drained the sink, the water gurgling loudly as it circled around and disappeared. She rinsed her hands of soap and took a clean dishcloth from a drawer by the stove. She moved unerringly, without thought. Wow. We'd been here long enough . . . *they'd* been here long enough . . . that it was second nature to grab a dish towel from a previously unknown drawer. This was becoming home to her.

And it had nothing to do with me.

"Let's go," urged Miles. "We need to make sure Tabby's okay."

"I can't leave," I whispered.

"You have to," insisted Miles. "Remember what you said. If Madame Arnaud takes Tabby, then your mom will have suffered two deaths."

I whirled around and looked at him. So cruel, such cruel words! But the kindness on his face reminded me that he was only parroting back what I had said.

One by one, Mom replaced the glasses and dishes in the cupboards, and pulled open a drawer to lay the silverware in their separate compartments. A lock of hair fell out of her too-short ponytail. She was still young for someone with a teenaged daughter. Correction: for someone who'd lost a teenaged daughter.

I let Miles wrap an arm around my waist and pull me

away from that most beautiful of sights, my gorgeous mom washing the counters. We went down the hall.

Tabby was in her crib as Steven sat in the armchair nearby, reading by the dim light of a lamp. It was one of those nights when she'd been fussy, maybe fighting off a cold—she just needed someone to sit in the room with her while she slept. I'd done it myself several times. It wasn't so bad, reading, listening to her light snore, and saying, "It's okay, I'm here; go back to sleep" when she'd periodically wake up.

So Miles and I relaxed. Madame Arnaud would never dare come to take Tabby while Steven kept vigil. Miles and I sat on the floor, talking. I twitched every time Steven turned a page.

"So how does Madame Arnaud see me?" I asked. "I'm a ghost to her."

"I don't know," said Miles. "I guess she's sensitive. A psychic or something."

"What are we going to do? We can't communicate with the living or even touch them."

"There has to be something, and we'll figure it out," said Miles firmly.

I had a funny thought. We'd tried for so long to re-trieve Eleanor Darrow's diary to show it to my parents; maybe it was time to retrieve Eleanor herself.

The next morning, Miles and I stayed close to my family. I knew he probably wanted to go home (or whatever verb now replaced *go* for us, to describe the way we simply *were* somewhere else instantly, the way you are in dreams). He doubtless wanted to see his mom and dad now that he knew the truth and everything had changed. I wasn't sure how long he'd been dead, or where he went when he wasn't with me, other than driving and re-driving that one stretch of road. Maybe he even wanted a moment with Gillian again, to try to find the closure she just couldn't give him.

But he stayed with me as I watched my family with a degree of fascination I'd never felt when I was alive. Every nuance of expression on Mom's face now left me slack-jawed with wonder and loss. As she walked from the counter to the table with milk for Tabby, I examined her with the same avid interest a lover would . . . the sway of her hips, the slight movement of her hair, the almost inaudible sigh she made as she sat.

The same with Steven. Although our stepdad-stepchild relationship had been a little troubled, suddenly I loved every stubbled inch of his face, the pale gray of his eyes, even the smears on his glasses that needed cleaning. I felt a bit of a draw back to my real dad, but couldn't bear to leave Mom.

And I felt a strong connection to Tabby. The sister I'd been exasperated with in life, who grabbed all my mom's attention right when I entered the tough years of puberty and needed her most . . . I wished I could go back in time and be nicer to her. I had smiled and sung and car-ried her . . . but lots of times I'd ignored her fussing as I sat inches away texting Bethany or Richard.

"I wish I could save you," I whispered.

"Don't start crying again," warned Miles. "Let's go find Eleanor like you suggested." He stood by Steven, who was eating his toast standing up, waiting for the coffeemaker to finish filling the carafe.

Before I'd realized I was dead, I would sit down at the breakfast table with them and somehow not notice that food never appeared for me—and neither did I want it. But now even sitting was a concept for the living. I just *was*.

"If we *can* do something, why has Madame Arnaud lived for hundreds of years?" I asked, as a way of delaying leaving. Tabby was here; she was safe. We could just stay and watch Mom. "All these servants walking around blaming themselves for not acting when they were alive—don't you think they'd have done anything they could afterward?"

Miles chewed on his lower lip. "The people who served in the last few centuries lived in a very different England. No access to education, and a lot of access to a class system that ensured they felt inferior. Perhaps they thought they were too powerless to even try."

"They've felt powerless for over two hundred years, some of them?" I asked in disbelief. "They have nothing to lose."

"You say that from a twenty-first-century perspective," he said. "Their lives—and apparently their deaths, I see—were very different."

As if to illustrate his point, one blundered in just then. She was slender to the point of emaciation, and her cap slumped over what must be a thinned collection of once-lush hair. She nervously ran her lye-reddened hands down the white field of her apron.

"Miss," she implored me. "I can't find Cook to get me orders."

"I . . . don't know," I said. I felt a cold jolt of sensation to be directly addressed by a ghost. I couldn't think of Miles that way, but she certainly fit the description. She was harried and upset, as ghosts are reputed to be, and in old-fashioned clothes to boot.

"But I've been sairchin' and sairchin' . . . nigh onto . . ." Her voice dwindled and I saw the horrifying realization cross her face that she'd been searching for Cook for centuries.

"See?" said Miles. "She's spending her afterlife trying to find someone to tell her what to do."

"Shh!" I said. "She can hear you!"

"She may never find Cook," he said. "Tucked away in the kitchens, the cook might've been oblivious to the evils of the house. When she died, she may have gone on to a peaceful place."

"I need her to get me orders," insisted the woman. "Mum says I mun do all I'm bid and more besides, for I can't lose me place. We'll all starve."

She and I froze in a searching survey of each other's faces. Pity filled me. She was troubled by the doings of the manor, enough to haunt it, and still obsessed about hunger in a household whose inhabitants were long dead. What did she see in my face?

"I'm Maud Pike, and me family has the farm out on the Stone Cross Way," she said to me. "Can't you help me?"

"You're forgetting something, Maud," said Miles.

"I'm forgetting summat?" she asked. "Oh, I'll be beaten!"

Miles raised an eyebrow at me.

"Your family can't starve," I said gently. "Remember?"

"Can't?" she repeated. "I'm to provide for wee Jackie and Michael, as they're years from being able to work, and poor Sampson is addled and unable, and Mum with her hands full, and Da dead these three years . . ." Her face changed. "No, no, dead far longer," she marveled to herself. "And didn't Mum marry again, to John the smith, who did her well, and there was enow to eat, e'en with the passel of new uns he had on her?"

I waited.

She burst into tears. "But she never forgot me, did she? I'd watch her cry and my hands would go through her."

Oh, I could relate to what she said. I glanced over at my own mom, talking Tabby into finishing her oatmeal by making her spoon into an airplane with a swirling route.

"And she died, too, and finally Jackie me favorite was an old man. All of 'em. For years, I watched, and their children, too, though I was nothing to 'em." She paused a long while. I didn't dare look at Miles, in case he said something and interrupted her. I realized he had done the right thing in pushing her to recall the once-acknowledged fact of her own death. "But here I stayed, didn't I, in the house that killed me."

Now I looked at Miles. The house killed her? Not Madame Arnaud?

"What did the house do?" I asked, as softly as I could.

"Well, it harbored the mistress, didn't it? Let her carry on with her terrible business."

I frowned over at Miles. "And that . . . killed you?" I hated to use the *k* word, but after all, she had used it first.

"The shame did." She lowered her head and the loose cap slid a bit farther down her forehead. Her eyelashes were the color of sand. Poor girl, there wasn't much to her.

It took me a while to figure out what she meant. Shame? The house? Huh? Then I understood. She'd committed suicide.

Tears rolled down her thin cheeks. "And I was meant to support them all," she said. "But I couldn't stand meself bringing a plate of cakes for the little ones *she'd* brung here. Made me just as much a monster as her."

She wiped her face with her apron. "Thank the saints for John the smith. Though I'd no notion of him for Mum afore I . . ." Her voice trailed off.

How awful. She didn't look that much older than me. In fact, maybe she was my age. And her wages were responsible for feeding a family of . . . I think she'd mentioned four or five names. The only thing I'd ever been accountable for was good grades on my report card. Even my competitive swimming was something I felt no pressure around.

"Didn't you try to fight?" Miles asked.

"Oh, there was some as tried," she said. "But the mistress outsmarted the lot."

Steven walked through Miles to refill his mug, underscoring how incredibly powerless we were. Without substance, how could we fight Madame Arnaud?

"Oh, the bell!" cried Maud, and she scurried off through the wall. Not only did she hear instruments of her indenture that we were not privy to, she apparently followed the floor plan of her day, walking through doors that had been walled up.

"You see what we're up against," said Miles.

I nodded. I inhaled a shaky breath. Now that the conversation was over, I realized how much it had unnerved me. I had just spoken with someone who died in the 1800s. And why was the manor suddenly full of her kind? Ghosts were everywhere now.

Somehow overnight the manor had populated itself with ghosts . . . it didn't make sense. Then, with a sick pang, I got it.

"Miles, the difference is us," I said. "I think the ghosts have always been here. It's just that now we can see them, because we know we're dead, too."

Before Miles and I understood we'd passed, we could interact only with those who were also unaware, like . . . well, like anyone too young to understand the concept of death. That toddler in the back garden.

Dressed in his 1700s breeches, that boy had spent centuries confused, with no one to tend him, help him, mother him. What a pure and utter hell. And he'd never emerge, because the idea of death had never been explained to him.

For over two hundred years, he'd been bewildered that his mother never came . . . that *nobody* came. Too young to care for himself, he'd turned crazy. He was feral.

I stood there thinking, rocked to the core.

I wasn't exactly sure how long I'd spent unaware that I was dead—not long. A few months, maybe: whatever time it took Mom and Steven to overturn their lives and escape to another country. I'd heard the doctor's diagnosis and pushed that knowledge down, down, down, as tight as clothes stuffed in a suitcase before you start trying to zip it. I'd heard, understood, and discarded. I'd started over, just as Mom and Steven had tried to.

But it had been so horrible—so upsetting to talk to Mom and not have her respond properly, or at all. I felt constantly ignored. It was a crazy stroke of luck—if you could call it that—that Miles had died around the same time I did. We had each other at least. And we'd helped each other reach that crucial understanding.

But now . . . Were Miles and I going to spend eternity like Maud? Powerless?

I positioned myself in front of Mom and used every bit of my strength and intention to try to reach her. "Mom, it's Phoebe. I'm right here!" I said. "You have to help Tabby by getting out of here."

I put my hands on either side of her face, even though my trembling fingers passed through her jaw. "Please, Mom, you *have* to hear me."

She shuddered.

I jolted back myself, startled.

"Goose walking over her grave," said Miles.

Her quiver did seem to show I'd breached the film between the living and the dead.

"She felt me somehow!" I said. Although it seemed impossible that anything in my world could ever be happy again, I did feel a surge of something close to excitement. If I worked on it, could I eventually communicate with Mom?

I tried again, hovering inches away from her face. I exhaled. If I had a breath, it went right into her mouth as she in turn inhaled. "It's Phoebe. It's me."

This time she didn't move, didn't register my presence. "It's me, Mom, it's me," I repeated.

Over the course of what was, to her, a day, I stuck with her like a second layer of skin. I pleaded with her to notice me as she finished up breakfast and washed the dishes, as she sang a song for Tabby and put her down for her nap. I followed her room to room, punctuated a discussion she had with Steven by chanting, "Tabby's in trouble." I was with her when Tabby woke up, I played with them, I talked myself into a fury. And the whole time Miles patiently stayed with me, although I knew he wanted to go hunt down Eleanor Darrow.

Finally, I gave up.

"It's not working," I said stupidly. "Maybe I just had beginner's luck the first time."

He took me in his arms and hugged me fiercely. It was so good to *feel* him. Thank God he was here.

"Maybe you could try Steven," he said. "Or even Tabby."

I wouldn't rule out anything, but my relationship with

Steven wasn't half of what I had with Mom. If anyone was going to pay attention to me from the other side, it'd be her. And Tabby—even if I could convey to her the complex idea that she should urge the family to leave, who was going to listen to a toddler?

"I mean, even if you're not as close to him, maybe he's more psychically sensitive," he added.

Good point. Some people saw ghosts—or said they did—and some didn't.

That night, as Steven sat changing channels on the old-fashioned TV, using a toaster-sized remote control, I sidled up next to him. I lay my head on his shoulder, which required me to hold it up myself. I reached up an arm and hugged him. Good old Steven. He'd made Mom a lot happier than my real dad did.

"Steven," I whispered. "It's me, Phoebe."

"I hardly think a whisper is going to work when out-right shouting in your mum's face didn't," said Miles. I shot him an angry look, but softened instantly when I saw how earnest he was. He wanted this to work. And really, he could be a hundred other places instead of here trying to save my sister. He hadn't even left to see his own family yet.

"You're right," I said. I sat upright, face-to-face with Steven, and firmly spoke his name.

Nothing.

"Steven, listen!" I moved so that my mouth was at his ear. "It's Phoebe."

But like Mom, he wouldn't respond. He stonily watched the TV as I tried again and again. The show was some sort of sitcom filmed in stark matte, with the actors doing pratfalls and making expressions directly at the camera.

"Can't tell half of what they're saying with those accents," he said to Mom, who smiled.

Ironic. Along with a cast of mobile-faced actors, I was doing my best to deliver lines to my family, unsuccessfully.

Miles and I swam again. It was after hours and the only lights were the ones framing the emergency exit signs. I realized we'd been here before when the pool was closed, but not understood the dimness.

"Damn!" I said. "We need to stay with Tabby. Bring us back."

"I didn't bring us here," said Miles.

"So, what . . . it's random?"

"Your guess is as good as mine."

I was in a black swimsuit with a halter neckline. I'd had it as a freshman and forgotten it in a locker room. I'd gone back the next day, but someone must have snagged it. Objects behaved so strangely here, offering a semblance of reality, like the clothes I'd thought Mom had unpacked and put in the dresser for me. I knew now the drawer was completely empty. My mind had just been filling in gaps for me, protecting me from the harsh truth that I didn't need clothes, that I was dead.

"Does it feel weird?" he asked. He meant because it was my first time swimming since understanding that I'd drowned.

I cupped water and brought it to my face. No panic. Water was water. I shook my head.

"The two places we always go have to do with our deaths," he pointed out. "I drove and drove that damn stretch of roadway until you made me turn right."

I nodded. "I wonder why I don't go to the pool I drowned in," I said. "Back in California." I looked at him and my eyes narrowed. "And why do *you* come to the pool?"

"And why do you ride with me?"

It seemed like a clue. Some force had wanted us to meet, to ally our forces.

"Someone or something is on our side," I said.

I swam to the edge and pulled myself out. Easy. If only I could've done that when dizziness threw stars in my eyes.

I tipped my head back and looked up at the skylight. "Night is falling," I said. "We need to get back to the manor."

Miles pulled himself out of the pool, water glistening down his firm biceps and triceps. Or was that just a trick of my death now, to retain some sort of link to reality? Did water really course down his body? How could we be wet or dry if we had no substance?

I reached up to pull my loose hair into a ponytail and wring it . . . but it was already dry. I looked at him. Dry now, too.

He pulled me to him and kissed me. It felt incredible—the best thing I'd felt in seemingly years. He put a hand on the small of my back and one on the back of my head, both gently pulling me toward him. Our bodies met, from toes to hips to forehead.

But now that I knew what I knew about us, the sensation was a little bit muted. His body seemed real to me; but it wasn't real.

I adjusted to find nuance, like a blind person develops greater hearing. Our bodies would do this for us . . . but not with the same roaring sensuality we'd been able to experience when alive.

We sank onto . . . well, a bed appeared. We were in a room. On the wall was a handmade wooden shelf with several trophies on it. The curtains were a striped brown and there was a desk with very messy piles of paper and textbooks on it, and a dresser.

"It's my room," said Miles.

Downstairs, we heard a TV. I looked at him questioningly. This was his chance to see his family again.

"I've been here before," he said. "Obviously I've been here before. But I mean, I've been here since the accident. There's the phone Gillian called me on," he pointed to an old-fashioned loaf-shaped phone on his desk, with a cord snaking into the wall, "to ask for a ride."

I sat up. As good as it had felt to kiss him, we had moved into a different mood.

"My folks watch TV endlessly," he said. "And I've tried to talk to them. Same as you, doubtless. Trying to convince myself that they were responding in a way."

"Do you want to go downstairs?" I asked. "I can wait for you."

"No," he said. "I can't."

I kissed a slow line of petite kisses along his jawbone. I ached for his sadness.

"I'm their only child, you see," he said. I buried my head in his shoulder. "That's why I want to make sure Tabby makes it."

Oh my God.

"You're incredible," I said. And I meant it. I'd known him for less time than any other guy I'd ever kissed, but his spirit was golden to me. Shimmering like it could break through his skin. What a good and pure soul. I was so lucky to have met him. He couldn't resolve his own parents' sadness, so instead he turned to help mine.

"You are, too," he said, giving me that slightly crooked, sexy smile. "I think we were meant to be together. We're like a posthumous Romeo and Juliet."

I laughed. "Well, Juliet only *pretended* to be dead the first time," I said. "And our families aren't fighting."

"You're so literary," he teased. "If you'd gone on to college, would you be an English major?"

I swallowed hard, all laughter gone. "Don't go down that road," I said. "We can't think about what might have been."

" 'Down that road.' That's funny," he said.

"Crap! Sorry."

He shrugged and ran a soft palm over my cheek. "We wouldn't have met if we weren't dead," he said. "You'd still be in California, right? Your parents only moved to get a fresh start and try to create a new life where there were no bad memories?"

I nodded.

"So the universe . . . or the antiuniverse . . . brought us together."

"Maybe we're also meant to take care of Madame Arnaud," I said. "Like you said, maybe that's what we need to do to 'graduate.' "

We kissed until I didn't hear the TV anymore, until I would have done anything for him.

He rose up from me. "No," I said, "Come back."

He gave me a long, reluctant look. "We should be thinking of Tabby," he said.

Ashamed, I nodded.

"We're so forgetful, like the way we couldn't ever seem to get back to that servant's chamber to fetch her diary," he mused. "It has to do with . . ."

"With our major problem regarding living?" I prompted with a wry smile.

"Yeah. It's like part of us is asserting our right to 'rest in peace,' but the other part knows we have to do something."

It made sense. Bit by bit, we were learning more about our condition. Death was like an upper level class. I needed Bethany to help me study for it.

Mortality 101.

Channeling my intention, I instantly moved with just a thought into Tabby's room. I rushed to her crib: empty. I looked around quickly, my heart thudding in my chest: her toys were all put away, and she was not playing anywhere here.

Oh please, God, I will never forgive myself . . .

I tried the living room.

She was there with Mom and Steven. She was sitting on the floor flipping pages of a board book, looking at the pictures.

Mom was in her robe, yawning, so it must be morning. Tabby had survived the night although I'd spent it on Miles's bed instead of protecting her.

But of course Madame Arnaud had left her alive. She wanted me to find someone else for her. My terrible task still lay ahead of me.

"Thank God, little sweetheart," I said. "I'm sorry." I bent down and kissed her, or the best I could do, on her forehead.

She stiffened.

Whoa.

I did it again, and she batted at me as if I were a fly.

Omigod.

So I could affect her! She felt me! A rush of joy came over me, and the sneaking feeling that maybe there was a way out of all this. If she could feel me, I could get through to her.

When I'd tried to take her from Madame Arnaud's arms, there'd been so much commotion I hadn't registered any reaction from her, simply my own failure to lift her or hold her.

"Tabby, it's Phoebe," I said. "Phoebe, Phoebe, Phoebe."

She didn't see me. She didn't react. Still . . .

I kissed her again and saw her eyebrows momentarily flicker into a frown.

"Anne, what's this on Tabby's arm?" asked Steven.

Standing next to me, he had noticed the puncture wound. *Nice one, Steven!* I loved the look of concern on his face. What a good man.

"I told you about it," Mom said. "I think there's an exposed nail in her crib. I thought you took care of it."

"I did look at the crib," said Steven. "But I didn't see *this.*"

He showed her the puncture wound, now with a vibrant yellow and blue bruise around it. Tabby must've pulled off the layers of Band-Aids that had previously covered it. I watched avidly as he ran his index finger over the injury. Tabby winced and pulled her arm away. "You think a nail caused this?"

"It's all I could think," said Mom. "It's looking awful."

"Is it from her last round of immunizations?"

"No, that was closer to her shoulder."

"Is she up on her tetanus shot? We don't have to worry about that, do we?" he asked.

"Oh, she's covered. She had to get every shot possible to get on a transatlantic flight."

They both looked at the wound, troubled . . . but not scared.

"Well, if this is the worst thing that happens to her, we'll be getting off pretty easily," Steven said.

Mom looked at him levelly. *Oh, don't go there!* I thought. I could tell she was going to start thinking about me. I represented the worst thing that could happen to a child.

"Sorry," he said. "Slip of the tongue."

"That's fine," she said, in a tone that was trying too hard to be bright.

"Tell them where it's from!" I said fiercely to Tabby.

"Lady drank," Tabby offered up. I gasped, but I wasn't sure if she was following my dictate, or simply reacting to the attention Steven was paying the bruise.

"Lay dee drank?" Mom laughed, kind of forcedly. I could tell she was doing her best to steer her mind away from the darkness of me. "Do you mean *la-di-da*?"

"Lady drank," Tabby repeated. "She use straw."

"That's right," Mom cooed delightedly. "We do use straws when we drink sometimes! Do you want a straw?"

"Okay," said Tabby.

Mom said excitedly, "She's getting so talkative! And the odd things she remembers. Straws, for Pete's sake. I'll get her some next time we're out."

"Could be a good way to transition away from sippy cups," said Steven.

And that was it. On to a new topic. They hadn't made the connection that Tabby was explaining about her injury. Lady drank: if only they had listened better! But what person in their right mind would ever reach the conclusion that someone was putting a straw in their child's arm to drink her blood? They put ointment on Tabby's wound and covered it with a fresh Band-Aid, all the while talking about language development and how Tabby was making great strides.

"She's learning faster than—" Mom started to say, but

then stopped. The only other toddler whose ability to talk she'd monitored was me, years ago.

I stayed with them for hours. My thoughts drifted to Miles, now that I was convinced Tabby was momentarily safe. Why had we been separated? I wished he was here right now, his chin rubbing against my temple as we together exulted over Tabby's ability to feel me.

I decided to try again. So Mom hadn't heard what Tabby was saying—the same way she didn't hear me, before or after my death—but maybe with different, simpler words it would work. I bent down to Tabby's level.

"It's me, Phoebe," I said. I kissed her forehead, then each cheek in turn. I loved to see how she slightly winced. She was aware of me all right. "Phoebe. Phoebe loves you."

I finally got something out of her after dozens of attempts.

"Phee," she said.

I was in the library, a few feet from the lectern that held the book on the Arnaud family history.

"Hell yeah!" said Miles. He ran and threw his arms around me. I reveled in his embrace and pulled his head down for a huge, lingering kiss.

"Oh my God," I said. There was no way to express the emotions he made me feel. He stepped back and held my face in both of his hands, looking at me as if I was the best thing he'd ever seen in his life. Or the best thing he'd ever seen in his death, I guess. There were those gold flecks in his eyes that I'd been longing to see again, buried deep in the blue of his irises. His jaw was covered with light stubble: did he have to ghost-shave here in our world? What determined how our bodies appeared when we didn't really have bodies?

We kissed again, and I paid attention to the drag of his whiskers on my skin. That felt real.

"I've been trying to bring you here for days!" he said.

"It's been days?" I frowned. "It didn't seem that long."

"I don't know," he said, frowning in turn. "Time is very . . . wiggly."

"Whatever, I'm so happy to see you," I said. "I missed you."

"You have no idea," he said. "I don't think I've ever wanted to see someone so much."

I felt a quiver of sensation straight to my gut. For a moment, my head clouded and I felt like I couldn't even think. "How'd you bring me?" I managed to ask.

"I just thought about you in so focused a way that I think it eventually pulled you. I'm getting better at it. Just before you came, I literally felt a tug like . . . I don't know, like there was a rope embedded in my chest and you were pulling it."

"I've felt that, too," I said. "After I realized I had drowned, I tried to reach you, and it felt like that."

He nodded. "That tug," he said. "It's you, or it's me, or it's something else."

"Right before you pulled me here, I got Tabby to say my name."

His eyebrows shot up in excitement, but he shook his

head. "Brilliant. The one person who is open to the idea of you is also the one who has the least authority."

"If I work on it, maybe I can coach her to say things," I said. "Get a message through to Mom."

"I'm sorry I pulled you away, then," he said. "You've been a lot more effective than I have."

"It's okay," I said. "It's worth it to see you. And she's safe now, with Mom and Steven."

"You look fantastic," he said, reaching out to touch my hair. "Never seen you in a ponytail before."

I almost couldn't bear the intensity of how his expression made me feel. I buried my face in his chest, needing to break the power of his gaze. His arms wrapped around me, and we stood there for a while just breathing together.

Our version of breathing, that is.

When I was calm enough to look at him again, his face looked thoughtful. The mood had shifted.

"Let's go," I said. "Let's see if Eleanor's in her room."

CHAPTER TWELVE

Constables broke up a fight at the Boot and Brick Pub yesterday, with Mr. Matthew Billcock suffering the brunt of injuries. He was treated by Doctor Wood at his dispensary and is in no serious danger. Billcock was set upon by Mr. Joseph Taylor and Mr. Andrew Wright, and witnesses say he offered up no fight, submitting to the beating. The dispute apparently arose over Billcock's masonry work at the Arnaud Manor. He is a sculptor, and his family, dating back to his great-grandfather, has fashioned funerary monuments for the Arnaud dead since the mid-1700s.

—*Grenshire Argus*, April 4, 1833

She sat on her bed, looking out the window. One finger hovered an inch from the glass, tracing the legend *Poor Little Babes*. Dressed in a long black dress with an equally long white apron over the front, she also wore a cap that covered most of her hair. Her face was pretty in a sober, sad way.

As we approached, she whirled around, I think just as frightened by our entry into her secret room as by our modern clothes.

"Eleanor," I said. "We need your help."

She stood up with a shriek that made me cringe. She dashed between us, out the little door.

"Wait!" called Miles. "Wait! We're against Madame Arnaud! We want to stop her."

She turned back around again, eyes blazing, to point her finger at me. "Looking the way she does?" she said defiantly. "I won't help you procure children."

"I told you," said Miles to me. "You look like Madame Arnaud."

Given Eleanor's reaction, I guess maybe he was right. "It's a coincidence," I said. "I'm not an Arnaud. But my sister is, and she's in danger."

She hovered in the doorway, ready to bolt if this was a trick.

"My family moved in here. They're still living. My sister's only two. Madame Arnaud has already . . . she's already . . ." I couldn't say the words. I looked at Eleanor helplessly. Her face showed compassion. I mustered the breath to continue. "We know you were brave. We saw what you . . . wrote . . ."

She frowned. *Oh.* We hadn't considered the reality of telling her we'd read her diary. To us it had seemed like a historic artifact, with no personality attached to it anymore. She might bristle, though, that we'd gone through her things.

"You read my diary?" she asked. "But how? We can't touch things."

She came back into the room and tried to pull her trunk back from the wall. Her hands went straight through it. Miles turned to me with narrowed eyes.

"I couldn't pull it back, either," he said. "What's different about you, Phoebe?"

"I don't know!" I moved the trunk, opened the secret drawer, and retrieved her diary, rifling through the pages.

I held it out to her and she couldn't take it. Her fingers, filmy and gray, passed through the red leather. Miles reached out a hand and his too went unfaltering through the volume as if it weren't there.

"You're special, miss," said Eleanor.

"Please don't call me that. My name is Phoebe." I hated the idea that she still felt part of the serving class, that she was somehow not on my level. "And this is Miles."

She nodded at both of us and stopped herself just on the edge of giving a curtsey.

"We didn't mean to violate your privacy," said Miles. "When we read it, we thought it was a hundreds-year-old volume that might help us understand how to defeat Madame Arnaud."

"It *is* a hundreds-year-old volume," she said, "and I forgive you for reading it. I haven't written in it for centuries. Please, sit."

She sat on the floor while we sat on her small cot. I looked down at her head, bowed in its starched white cap. This wasn't right. Almost of one accord, Miles and I slid down to the floor next to her. It was worth it to see the look pass through her eyes.

"So, please tell us what you know," Miles said.

"There's one thing I didn't write down in my diary," said Eleanor. "Because I was, shall we say, *separated from my life* before I got the chance to chronicle my deed."

She paused.

"I tried to kill Madame Arnaud. I stabbed her in her bed one night."

Whoa.

"Nice one," murmured Miles.

I wanted to hug her. She'd taken action—and apparently died for the risk she took. "What happened?" I asked.

"I was her lady's maid and therefore entrusted with all kinds of duties in her bedchamber. I waited one night until she fell asleep, and then I stabbed her with my knife." She looked at us with pale gray eyes. "I made sure she was dead. I stabbed hard. The mattress was ruined beneath her."

I sucked in my breath. Madame Arnaud had written about this—the bed had been filled with swan feathers.

"But yet she lives," she continued.

"When she awoke," I said, "there was no blood. She only saw the knife and the cut mattress."

"Aye," she said. "There are magical forces that protect her. The house returned the blood to her."

"The house?" exclaimed Miles.

I watched her face avidly. This was not a new idea to me, that the house was in collusion with Madame Arnaud. For a second, I saw how it might have happened, the mattress plumped with blood like a sponge, and how it would roll her over and drip into her half-open mouth, replenishing her.

"There are dark forces at work in the manor," Eleanor said. "I used to talk quite a bit with the stable hand Austin, who thought it was built on a pagan site. His mother knew a lot of the lore, and he shared it with me. They still call this Auldkirk Lane?"

"Yes," I said.

"Auldkirk means 'old church.' "

Miles nodded. "Of course. I'd noticed that but never thought about it before."

"We think the manor was built on a pagan ritual site, and that Madame Arnaud's evil is somehow connected with the ancient powers here," she said.

"Is Austin still around?" asked Miles.

She shook her head. "I've looked for hundreds of years. If he's here, I can't reach him."

"What happened when you stabbed Madame Arnaud? I mean, what happened to *you*?" I asked.

"It looked like she had died, and I congratulated myself on such a tidy job. Why had no one tried to do it before, I thought, with myself so brave. I went to my bed; practically singing in the hallways, I was. We were all released!"

She straightened the lines of her apron. While Miles and I sat Indian style, casually, she was kneeling to protect her outfit.

"The next morning, I woke to hear the house at its customary business, and the girl who laid Madame Arnaud's fire chattering about some dream Madame Arnaud had told her about. She had lived through being stabbed. Not just stabbed: pinned to her mattress by my knife. I was in despair, and knew she would torture me for my treachery. So I left service immediately."

"You did well," I said earnestly. "I'm surprised you're still . . . here. You shouldn't be plagued by guilt like all the other servants are."

"Oh, I'm plagued nonetheless," said Eleanor. "And

I'm not the only one. I had heard rumors throughout the years that madame had survived at least several other attempts on her life."

"Stabbing didn't work," said Miles. "What will?"

She gave us a very, very, very old smile. A smile that expressed the centuries she had spent wishing for something that just wasn't possible. "Nothing will."

"I don't believe that," said Miles.

"You're dead," she said. "You can't hold a weapon. And you can't fight the house's power."

"Phoebe holds things," he pointed out.

"What else do you know about the original pagan site here?" I asked.

"Not much. It may have been a place of sacrifice, which makes sense because of spilled blood. Austin said there was once a powerful yew tree on the estate somewhere, the source of power."

"You never found it?"

"No. I think it had been cut down by villagers who feared its strength."

Miles whistled between his teeth. "I just thought of something," he said. "She's essentially a vampire, right? Except still alive instead of undead? What if we used garlic or . . . what is it, a silver bullet?"

"A silver bullet is for werewolves. You're thinking of a wooden stake," I said. "But I don't think she's a vampire."

"I don't know this word," said Eleanor. "But I believe Madame Arnaud tapped into the unholy properties of blood that can be unlocked for some. Have you heard of the medieval Hungarian woman Elizabeth Báthory?"

"No," I said.

"She bathed in the blood of virgin peasants to keep her skin fresh and youthful. She also, if the victim was beautiful, drank the blood."

"Sounds familiar," said Miles.

"She even began a young woman's academy to ensure a fresh crop of women," said Eleanor. "She is blamed for the deaths of six hundred women."

"But did she extend her life, like Madame Arnaud has?" I asked.

"Perhaps she might have, if she had continued her foul practice," said Eleanor. "Her crimes were discovered and she was imprisoned like an anchorite in her own castle. She died four years later. Being away from the source of her power for that long a time could explain her death."

Miles looked at me. "How long has it been since Madame Arnaud has entertained a young visitor?"

"Madame Arnaud drank from Tabby," I reminded him. "She didn't drink everything, thank God, but she drank something."

"Of course," he apologized. "I'm sorry. How could I forget?" His hand on his thigh formed into a fist.

"It's okay," I said. "There's so much going on."

Eleanor looked thoughtful. "Madame Arnaud must be weak now from years of not feeding—until recently, of course. But she isn't helpless, not by a long stretch.

"Miss . . . I mean, Phoebe, you can touch and hold things?" asked Eleanor.

I cast my mind back, cataloging the things I'd been able to touch in the manor.

It wasn't that I had been paralyzed in trying to select a pen to undertake the automatic writing . . . it was that I had tried and not been able to. Much like trying to touch Tabby, I had attempted to pick up a pen and my fingers had drifted through it. I had somehow blocked that out because it didn't jive with my version of reality. But now I remembered: my hand sank through the pencils until it came to rest on the solid wood of the desk. I *could* touch the desk.

What was the rule here? I could put a hand on existing elements of the house, but not modern things or things my family had brought?

I hadn't been able to touch Steven's printer or the paper in its tray. If Madame Arnaud hadn't fanned the pages out for me so each was visible, I wouldn't have been able to read them. And when I'd tried to gather them up to show Mom and Steven . . . that's when I had suffered one of those time blips. My mind was rebelling from the confusion of not being able to touch them.

"I'll be right back," I said to Miles and Eleanor.

I *focused,* just the way I'd once called Miles to me. I gave over all my intentions and suddenly I was where I wanted to be, back in Steven's den. I tried the pencil cup and printer again: untouchable. I walked back out into the hallway, constantly testing my ability to touch. Paintings on the wall, furniture, lamps: all these things had texture and weight for me. But Steven's briefcase? No.

I walked down the hall, skirting a few servants who gave me wide berth and curtseyed as they passed.

Tabitha's crib, which had been here from the manor's original nursery furnishings? Yes.

Her blanket from home? No.

I smiled to myself. I could touch things: *Arnaud* things. That could be very helpful in the fight. But the smile instantly dropped from my lips.

I was remembering the night I'd watched the shadow show in the nursery. Another horrible truth my mind had protected me from.

That night, like Eleanor, I had been brave. I had tried to pick up my sister, and my hands went straight through her. I'd tried to push Madame Arnaud away, and my hands were made of air.

"Please . . . leave her alone," I'd pleaded.

Madame Arnaud had simply laughed. "I think not," she'd said.

In that complete and utter helplessness I'd sunk to my knees and watched the shadows playing on the wall. I had *tried*.

I returned to the two in Eleanor's room.

"—and her eyes," Eleanor was saying.

They both jumped when I reappeared. "What were you saying?" I asked.

"Nothing, miss," Eleanor said. "What did you learn?"

I didn't correct her using the honorific "miss" for me this time, as I had the uncomfortable feeling they had been talking about me.

"I can touch things original to the house," I said. "But not Madame Arnaud herself."

"If you can use a weapon, all that matters is that the weapon touch her, right?" Miles asked.

"But I stabbed her clean through," said Eleanor, "and all for naught."

We sat there in silence.

What could we do? I knew elsewhere in the house, Madame Arnaud made her way through lavishly appointed rooms, with the gleam of gold everywhere, and filigreed sconces and heavy velvet festooning her windows. Like a spider fat with silk, she crept to her sofa and perched on a cushion.

"If we can't kill her," I said slowly. "Maybe we can make her kill herself."

Miles looked up. He flashed a grin that made Eleanor gasp. Oh dear. I looked at her in dismay. Was she falling for him?

"What are you thinking?" he asked.

"An eighteenth-century woman probably doesn't know how to swim," I said.

Miles's face registered the plaintive knowledge that I had died in the water. Eleanor, however, simply looked reflective.

"She doesn't," she announced.

CHAPTER THIRTEEN

In the town of Grenshire, a local legend talks about
an immortal blood-drinker in the abandoned eighteenth-
century manor house on the outskirts of town. My interest in
the subject is personal, as an ancestor of mine worked in the
home as a lady's maid. Empty for many years, the castlelike
building begs for an official paranormal investigation, but access
isn't easily granted. The story goes that a woman
named Yolande Arnaud . . .

—From *Not At All Resting in Peace: Ghost Stories of England,
Scotland and Wales,* by Kate Darrow

"She doesn't know how to swim," continued Eleanor. "She hosted parties on the Grand Canal outside. She wouldn't so much as dip a toe in, although she encouraged others to."

"So we could somehow get her to water, and . . . well, we can't push her in," said Miles.

"There's a well in the cellars," said Eleanor eagerly. "For many years it was the sole source of water for the house."

I pictured the dank stone well in the vault of the manor and shuddered. "No," I said. "Something far outside the house's influence. Even the Grand Canal is too close."

Eleanor closed her eyes, thinking. "It's been so many

years," she said. Suddenly she brightened. "There's a woodland pool an hour's walk away," she said. "Austin said they used to refresh the horses there after a long ride."

"Let's look at it," I said.

She rose to standing and began walking to the door.

"No," I said. "We can go faster than that." I smiled at her while Miles explained the concept of moving with intention.

"I see," she said. "I am willing to try." She touched her cap as if she expected a big wind would come with our movement.

"You know the place," I said. "You visualize it, and you bring us there."

She nodded, and the sides of her mouth downturned for a moment. "To think I've wasted all this time," she murmured. "I've been stuck in the old ways of thinking about my body. Walking, even if through walls sometimes. Stuck here in this foul place."

I reached out and hugged her. She stiffened for a moment, then her arms crept around me, too. She sniffed.

"Are you all right?" I asked, pulling back.

She blinked back tears. "I haven't felt another soul in all these years," she said. "I see the other servants, of course, but we don't talk. We're all on our own miserable courses."

Miles stepped forward and hugged her, too, and this time I saw her hobnailed boots take a step backward. This was a lot to ask of her: not only shedding her ideas of class, but of gender, too. A male would never touch a female in this way in her era. "It's going to be just fine," said Miles to her softly. She looked up into his eyes. He smiled, and I watched her melt. Just as with me, her arms stole around his body to return the embrace.

I waited. Did this hug last a little too long?

I wanted to slap myself. This didn't matter. Nothing mattered except saving Tabby.

"To the woodland pool!" I said loudly.

Instantly, we were there.

Cobalt water slumbered under a floor of lily pads, so profuse and close together that they nearly hid the water altogether. Many of the lilies proffered a vertical shaft: a bud about to flower. It made the pond seem like a miniature forest.

Around the edges of the water, thick greenery. Trees so overgrown that they were wreaking havoc on themselves, one branch struggling for light beneath the canopy of its brother. A dock, fallen into disrepair, led a short way out into the middle.

I studied the scene.

"The lily pads are good," said Miles. "They hide the depth."

I looked at him, wanting to kiss him. He was exactly right!

"I have an idea," I said. "I'll be right back."

I took myself back to the Hansel and Gretel door, the part of the house where Madame Arnaud actually lived.

I knew from looking through the grate on the roof that this part of the house was furnished, that she spent her days here in relative comfort.

I turned the gray stone that constituted a doorknob. I was in an entrance hall, smaller in scope than the grand entrance of the main wing, but still impressive . . . and filled with color. Somehow furniture hadn't molded here, wasn't furred with dust. There were all kinds of sofas for guests to sit upon and remove their outerwear, to hand over to a maid. Little tables to hold the glass of wine offered upon arrival.

I went to the window, covered with powder blue curtains embroidered with gold thread in a fleur-de-lis pattern. I pulled.

Noise from behind me.

I whirled around.

Nothing there.

Nothing I could *see.*

I thought of something horrible. I knew Madame Arnaud preferred children as young as possible, to imbibe their futures. I knew she often chose babies. I had never seen a baby ghost, perhaps because they were all here in this wing of the house where they'd died.

Adrenaline surged through my body. This wing must be filled with babies, crawling on the floors, or maybe even too young to do *that,* unaware that they had died. Thank God I had never been inside this part of the house before I understood that I was dead. I don't think I could bear that sight. Yet . . . I knew they were here.

I turned back around and tugged at the curtain in earnest. I needed it. I had to release those babies.

Another noise.

Was Madame Arnaud behind me? All I had to do was get this curtain down and return to the pond. She wouldn't be able to follow me; she couldn't travel as I did. The one benefit to being dead.

The curtain rod above me squealed with the pressure, and I leapt, using all my body weight to pull down the fabric. The rod broke, and the curtains came to the ground, pooling into elegant ripples.

"Whatever are you doing?" came her voice. Ice formed all over my back. I bent to release the curtains from the rod. *She can't hurt you,* I told myself. *You tried to touch her once, and your hands went through her. You'll be fine.*

The rod was heavy, and the curtains so massive that I fought to pull them off the end.

"I asked you a question." She was only a few yards behind me now.

Oh my God. Just do it, just pull!

Now I had lost the rod within the volume of fabric. I continued to yank, but wasn't sure I was pulling in the right direction. I stepped to the side, and the curtains came with me. Were they free, though? I threw the handful to the side and grabbed a new section to pull.

"My dear."

She had whispered in my ear. I could see her in my peripheral vision, black hair in an extravagant concoction, piled atop her head à la Marie Antoinette. The jewels around her neck caught a wink of sunlight from the now-bared window and momentarily blinded me.

I froze.

"A common thief, taking my curtains," she said. "But you may have them. In exchange for something, of course."

Her voice was so foreign, her English spoken with an overtone of ancientness, of French, of something else. The curtains fell from my hands.

"I have told you already what I desire," she said. "A new child."

I nodded.

"Oh please," she whispered. "Something good. With fat, ruddy cheeks. I want to see blood in its face."

I nodded again.

"Look at me," she commanded.

I closed my eyes.

"You couldn't touch your sister," she continued. "You couldn't touch *me*. But look at you, pulling down festoons of curtains. Touch a child for me. Bring a child to me. And I will let your sister go."

"Forever?" I said.

"Of course," she whispered.

"All right," I said. My eyes still closed, I listened as she left, those skirts rustling as they had in the hallway the night she had drunk from my sister.

When I opened my eyes, the curtains lay folded in a neat pile at my feet.

CHAPTER FOURTEEN

The *Grenshire Argus* announces the death of Miss Maud Pike,
aged 18, on the 15th of August. Well-loved by her family, Miss
Pike recently undertook employment in the kitchens of the
Arnaud Manor. She returned home for her Sunday visit, and
evidenced a distressed demeanor. The next morning as her
brother readied the carriage to return her, he found her in the
family barn, hanged. She is survived by her mother, Mrs.
Elizabeth Pike, and her three siblings, Jack, Michael, and
Sampson. Services will be held at St. Augustine Parish
at 2 o'clock tomorrow.

—*Grenshire Argus* obituary, August 16, 1842

*T*hat night, we retired to Tabby's room to talk over our plans. We knew none of us were eligible for sleep, and this way I could keep an eye on my sleeping sister. In the dim glow of her night-light, we sat in a circle on the floor and rehearsed the strategy.

"You and Miles should hide in the trees along the far side of the pond," I said.

"Whatever for?" asked Eleanor.

I steeled myself to not react as if she were stupid. It was like Miles had said: the working class of the 1800s was not educated.

"So that Madame Arnaud can't see you," I said.

She laughed. "She can't see us!" she said. "She's never seen any of the servants, nor any of the children." She glanced over at Miles. They shared a look, and I knew they had been talking about me while I was away fetching the curtains.

"I don't see the resemblance," I said flatly. "She has black hair, mine is auburn."

"It's in your facial structure and your eyes," said Miles.

"Don't you see it's the only explanation that makes sense?" Eleanor said gently. "You can touch the things of this house, because they're yours by inheritance. She can see you—and only you—because you're of her line."

"My real father is Don Irving," I said. "He lives in Phoenix and *he* has auburn hair. Steven is my stepfather."

"Your mom's hair is auburn, too," said Miles softly.

"Look—what does it matter? What if Steven was my real dad?"

"It matters a lot," said Eleanor. "You're the eldest. If you hadn't died, you would be heir."

I snorted. "This clunky barfhouse would be mine?" But I realized she was serious.

"It also means you have a very special relationship to Madame Arnaud."

I looked over at Tabby, slumbering slightly above my eye level in her crib. Not my half sister, but my real sister? Steven had been on the scene *very* soon after my parents divorced. Was it at all possible he had been in Mom's life for years already at that point—truly my father?

"This is really weird for me right now," I mumbled.

Miles leaned over and nudged my shoulder, knocking me off balance. Eleanor looked horrified as I fell to my elbow; males and females didn't behave this way in her day. "Let's see," he said. "You found out you were dead, that your house has ghosts and an immortal blood-drinker, that your sister is being stalked, and for a while you thought you were crazy. Weird is your world, baby."

I didn't get up, but stayed there half perched. I laughed. "Oh my God," I said. "Weird doesn't even begin to describe it."

We held each other's gaze as we laughed for what seemed like twenty minutes. After a while, Eleanor joined in with a tentative giggle. I collapsed fully onto my back and let myself roar. My diaphragm started to hurt from laughing so hard.

"And we don't even know what comes next," I said.

We all abruptly stopped.

Chapter Fifteen

Elsie Harlow, 32, who recently relocated to Grenshire from her native London to take up service at the Arnaud Manor, is dead by her own hand this 30th June. Little is known of her, and the constabulary request assistance with determining next of kin for notification.

—*Grenshire Argus*, July 1, 1856

I was looking for Madame Arnaud. I climbed luxurious, curving stairs in her wing of the house. I passed the statue of a lion on the landing, roaring and clawing the air in some fit of marble pique. On one landing, a coat of arms showed three gold crowns on a field of blue.

Servants passed me, some aggrieved, one who gave me a wink. "We should've helped them," I heard the whisper going round. "Why did we do nothing?"

I walked down the hall, stopping to look in each door. These were the kind of rooms I'd dreamed about as a girl: made for royalty, with enormous canopy beds and marble fireplaces with shepherdess figurines cavorting on the mantel, and overstuffed armchairs to sit and read in.

Candelabra sat atop carved cabinets to hold all one's delicious princess belongings.

Eleanor had told me Madame Arnaud's chambers were on the second floor, and had instructed me which door to look for. Murals covered the walls, 1700s men and women frolicking at a picnic, winding flirtatious hands around the rope of a swing hung from a tree, skirts and hat ribbons flouncing. Their cheeks were red from wine drinking and their painted smiles were greedy. Remembering that Miles thought Madame Arnaud modeled the back lawns after Versailles, I wondered if they were the nobles of that famous palace, who never worked and only played—knowing bread and cakes would always be provided by someone else's labor. Every few feet, glossy white doors interrupted their revels.

A girl, probably seven, crouched in one of these doorways, holding her arm with a cross expression. As I walked past, I noticed the thin line of gray blood seeping from under her hand. "It hurt," she whimpered to me.

"I'm so sorry," I said. "I'll get her back for you."

An Americanism she didn't understand?

"I mean, I'll make her pay," I amended.

She grinned up at me, and I winced to think that her family had been deprived of that sunshine.

I found Madame Arnaud's door, with her initials YA created in serpentine iron on the front. I knocked.

"*Entrez,*" she called.

I walked into an abattoir, a slaughterhouse. That's what it looked like anyway: red walls, red curtains, red Moorish carpets overlapping each other.

"Here you are," she purred. "Just when I was getting thirsty."

She sat in an armchair, tall as a throne. It was the healthy, beautiful version of Madame Arnaud. She was striking, with jewels sparkling in her dark hair. Her skin pale as muslin, her eyebrows dramatic arches above the wet slickery of her eyes.

"I have someone for you," I said.

"Tell me."

My attention was diverted by the table next to her. On it, the silver straw reposed on a tray, with a glint of light hitting it and creating a sparkle of luminosity.

It was a piece of artistry—the silversmith had made something beautiful out of something gruesome. The terminus of the straw was sharpened, like an old-fashioned pen nib, and a simple cylinder stretched out of the tip. But the portion closest to the drinker, to Madame Arnaud's lips . . . that was designed with fetching swirls of rococo flourishes, curled in upon itself, then flaring out in an asymmetric flurry.

I had seen it before, of course, but had suppressed that memory.

She surveyed my face. "Who do you have for me?" she prompted.

"A girl of seven," I said. "I couldn't find younger. She's robust and quite plump."

I waited for her to ask me her name. Eleanor had chosen it. My experience from my creative writing class was put to use in creating this phantom victim, but Eleanor had insisted on naming her.

"How did you procure her?"

"I told her about the organ, of course." Madame Arnaud would understand this reason, as she herself had used it. But no child today would care about playing an organ, nor necessarily know what one was.

"She's from the village?"

"Yes. I walked her here."

"Well, bring her in!"

I hesitated. "I had to leave her outside. I built a trap for her."

Madame Arnaud stared at me. For an unnerving second, I thought she saw through the plot.

"How resourceful of you," she said. "It is too blatant for my taste; I prefer promises of sweet things and favors so that they will come willingly, but I give you credit for ensuring her compliance."

I nodded.

"You're afraid if you open the trap, she will run?" she asked.

"Yes."

She sighed. "In the old days, any manner of servants would be available to fetch her."

"I think it best if you come with me," I said.

"Is it far?"

"It's very far," I said. "I'm sorry."

She pulled up her skirts and showed me the fragile slippers seemingly made of tissue. "Bring me the brown ones," she said imperiously, pointing toward her wardrobe.

I was tempted to say, "I'm not your lady's maid," but I wanted her to accompany me. I went over to the large wooden wardrobe and opened it. Inside rows of shoes stood, toes pointed out. Only one pair was brown, leather with stripes of fur that appeared to be fox, and they were indeed sturdier.

I brought them to her. She refused to take them, merely sat with her skirts pulled up. I knelt at her feet and exchanged the shoes for her. Her bare feet were horrible, thin, pallor-less. The veins, carrying too much blood, rose bloated and prominent from her skin.

"Fine, then," she said. "Do I need a wrap?"

"No," I said. "The winds have died down."

As we tried to leave the chamber, her door wouldn't open. *It's the house,* I thought. *It knows somehow.*

I stepped aside. "Can you open this?" I asked her.

She stood with one arm straight up, curved at the elbow, and made a motion with her fist. The door immediately opened, with such force that it banged into the wall. She glanced at me to see my reaction. I kept my face bland, although I was screaming inside.

The walk to the pond was an hour, Eleanor had told us, but it seemed like minutes, as we drifted through copse after copse and forlorn meadow after abandoned field. I almost thought Madame Arnaud was gliding, as I glanced back at her once.

Soon enough, I could see the pond ahead of us. "Ah, the site of some of my trickery," she said.

I whirled around to see a sly smile on her face. My heart began to pound. Did she know it was also the site of *my* trickery?

"She's there," I blurted out, pointing.

Sitting at the end of the dock, there was a cage I'd created out of branches and tree-fall. Inside it, the figure of a girl slumped. She was made of those thick curtains artfully arranged. I had worried Madame Arnaud would recognize the print, so I'd dyed them by soaking them in the murk and mud by the water's edge.

Madame Arnaud inhaled, and I was reminded of Steven's face when he would stick his nose into a wineglass and inhale.

"Nothing," she said.

"Nothing?"

"I don't smell her. All I can smell is this terrible brackish water. It's disgusting."

"Well, she's yours." I couldn't believe I had said something so horrible. I turned to Miles in tacit apology. He gave me a kindly look. He and Eleanor were standing there guarding the faux girl in a cage, although there was nothing they could do. They couldn't touch her.

Together Madame Arnaud and I walked down the dock. I'd created a large hole in its flooring, then covered it up with lily pads to look like they had just drifted over from the water. It was a low-lying dock, and water touched its edges.

I could scarcely breathe as Madame Arnaud walked closer to the cage. "Why did you trap her here?" she turned her head to ask. "Such a strange—"

She fell through the hole, just as she was supposed to. There was a tremendous splash, and water plunged up to set the cage rocking. She was simply gone. I rushed to the hole and peered down. I couldn't see her, but the water was dark. We waited.

"Oh my sweet Savior!" said Eleanor. "That was too easy."

"I know," said Miles. "Is she playing with us?" His face was paler than usual—now that I knew he was dead, his skin had taken on a grayish tint for me—and I saw him looking into the water nervously. I realized Miles had never seen Madame Arnaud before. Her presence as she stood on the dock in her bell-like skirts must have been formidable for someone who was new to the sight.

"What do we do now?" asked Eleanor.

"Wait. Count. No one can hold their breath for more than two or three minutes, especially if not trained."

I heard a sound that made my heart sink. A splash.

I looked to the right of the dock, where her head appeared. Her coiffure was undone and her hair created a pool of ink around her face.

"Help me," she cried pitifully.

She was struggling to stay afloat, but she had no idea what to do. She flailed, trying to maintain eye contact. She started to say something else, but sank down under the surface.

"What if . . . what if she swims under the lily pads where we can't see, and gets to the shore?" asked Eleanor. "We'd never know."

I realized she was right. The lily pads had seemed like a tool for us, but they could also be used to Madame Arnaud's advantage.

"I should go down there and make sure she drowns," I said.

"No, Phoebe!" said Miles adamantly.

"It's okay, I swim really well as long as I don't faint. And I don't think I can faint anymore."

"I've a better idea," said Eleanor. "Take a stick and stir the lily pads. We can see her from up here."

"The water's too dark," I said, shaking my head.

"I'm not letting you in there," said Miles.

"*Letting* me?"

"Eleanor's right. If she can get her feet under her, she can creep through here and we'd never see her."

"Phoebe, please don't go into the water," pleaded Eleanor.

"Please," said Miles.

"She can't hurt me," I said. "She can't even *touch* me."

"She'll figure something out," said Miles.

"This is all too easy," said Eleanor again, worried.

"I want to make sure she dies," I said. "Do you think if she gets out of here, she'll even *hesitate* to kill Tabby?"

I put my arms together above my head in a pose I hadn't struck in a long time—not since everything had changed—and dived into the water.

An interesting sensation. I could feel the cool of the pond's temperature, but I didn't need to hold my breath. I guess if I thought about it, it had been this way when swimming with Miles, but I just hadn't noticed, wasn't picking up the subtle nuances of life after death.

The water was indeed dark, and I swam below looking for signs of the waterlogged skirts. Above my head lolled the lilies, blocking the light, forming a curved, circular mosaic. For a moment they induced a mild panic: Would it be hard to surface? Would the house's evil knit them closely together so that I wouldn't be able to get through?

I didn't need to surface to breathe, I reminded myself, and I could use intention to be anywhere, anytime. In fact, I hadn't needed to dive into the water. I could've just *been* there.

I turned my head to the side, and there she was. Her pale face like an underwater moon, her body in those flayed, voluminous skirts like black pirate's sails unfurled from the rigging. She was after me.

I floundered backward. She knew I had spelled her doom, and wanted to revenge herself as best she could before her air ran out.

Although I couldn't feel it, she pressed her face to mine. I couldn't move. I had to listen to her litany.

She whispered incantations against my cheek, spiteful charms, monstrous fairy tales uttered into my skin. Her lips were moving, casting spells, damning me. She rained imprecations down on my head, unheard words given to the water, horrible spite and ancient vows long forgotten, old fireside-shadowed hatred.

I tried to swim away, but she came with me. She raised one white finger into the air, signaling me to wait, then she rose to the surface to catch a breath, flailing. She wasn't good at floating, but she was managing.

What do I do now?

I had led her to what I thought would be her death. She was in water over her head, and yet she wasn't drowning.

As she descended to me again, her skirts elegantly and slowly turned inside out, like a jellyfish I'd seen long ago in the Monterey aquarium. I couldn't be here. I had to get out. I looked for the supports of the dock, but didn't see them. Instead, I surged toward the deeper part of the woodland pool. Maybe she would follow me.

I swam the breaststroke, but clumsily. What did technique matter? I just wanted to get away from her and whatever spells she was casting.

All of a sudden, looming in the water ahead of me was a massive shape I first took for a gigantic fish. Then I saw it for what it was: the remains of a tree that had been cut down. Its profuse branchwork was like a heart underwater, veins and arteries sprawled across my vision. I swam down to see the cuts of the ax, now furred with algae, that had separated it from the stump, erratic and varied, as if many men had banded together, in panic, to fell the tree.

The stump was still there, separate, so large I could lie down on it should I wish.

They had cut it down and then flooded the site. This wasn't a naturally occurring pond. They had made it happen, by digging ditches to irrigate, by bringing water by the cartload. They had buried the tree with water.

As Madame Arnaud appeared in the gloom, I swam closer to the tree and its sense of protection. She followed me. *She's a fool for doing that,* I thought. *She should steer clear.*

Madame Arnaud touched a branch and her hair somehow reached around to snag itself on it. I watched her try to swim up. It was time for her to take a breath, but the tree held her hair.

She tugged with both hands at her own long, wanton hair—but her sleeve got caught by a twig. She fought to get it back.

Oh yes, this was a powerful tree.

Despite everything, her face made me want to weep. She needed a breath desperately. I had not been aware of the need for breath when I drowned: I had fainted, been in a state of hazy gladness as the stars took over my mind, constellations pinning me with each strident spark. It was hard to see on her face what might have been on mine. I nearly reached out to help untangle her from the tree's trap.

Her skirts drifted again with water pushing up from underneath, fanning them out. I saw without surprise how they snagged on another branch. She was caught, stretched out from limb to limb. The tree was a web, and she was a fly.

A glow arose and I swam closer. There was a symbol on the tree's trunk, now shining. *What is that?*

Another lit up. They were strange, but simple signs. *Runes.*

This was the pagan yew Eleanor had talked of. They had cut it down for fear of its power.

Madame Arnaud looked at me with despair. *Help me,*

she mouthed. A rune lit up right above her head. Some word from an ancient peoples, something I'd never understand.

I can't, I mouthed back.

Her face closed down in a black scowl, and I knew she couldn't make it a second longer. I rose to the surface, breaking free of the claustrophobia to arrive in a world with a real sky staggering with stars. It had turned night while we were underwater, and Eleanor was sitting on the edge of the dock crying, while Miles was standing on shore, his back to me, hands on his hips, looking in despair even if I couldn't see his face.

"Miss! You're alive!" Eleanor scrambled to her feet, while Miles raced to the dock.

"Oh my God, *no,*" I said, pulling myself up out of the water. It felt amazing to do it. I was not the one drowning this time. "Not alive. Not ever again. But *here.*"

She hugged me, and I wondered briefly if she would feel the wet and the cold or if her apron would be dry when we disengaged. But I forgot to check, because Miles was there putting his hand on either side of my jaw and snarling at me.

"Why the bloody hell were you down there so long?"

"We were having a tea party," I said. "Rude to leave early."

He didn't want to laugh. Oh, he was so mad. But he did. He let loose a reluctant, loud laugh.

"Miles, there's a *good* force here, too. I think the house is malevolent. But something brought us together, something kept sending you to your car and me to the pool.

It wanted us to figure things out and fix things. There's something good. Eleanor," I said, turning to her, "I think it's the pagan tree down there. Chopped down. It has glowing runes on its trunk."

"And where's Madame Arnaud?" she said.

"She's snagged in the tree," I said. "She's gone."

"Are you sure? We didn't think she could swim, and she gave that a good go, didn't she?" said Miles.

"There's no way she could hold her breath that long," I said.

We all three turned and surveyed the surface of the pond. Miles and Eleanor were expecting her head to break the water, but I knew the tree was holding her fast. "See?" I said. "Even if we started counting now, it's already been way too long. She couldn't survive."

I walked off the dock and emerged out onto the grass. Cool night air blew through my wet hair. Stars still held a modicum of light while the moon was queen of the sky, clutching at the crown half slipped from her head.

I wheeled around in a large and slow circle. I was exhausted to my core, but elated. I had fought water and won this time.

More important, I had vanquished the woman no one else could.

I had done it.

CHAPTER SIXTEEN

Silversmith Joseph Harcutt is grieved by his wife, Mary, and
two children, Elizabeth and Joseph, Jr. A third child, Grace,
predeceased Mr. Harcutt by one week. Known throughout the
county for his beautiful handiwork, Mr. Harcutt's greatest
accomplishment was fashioning a silver service for Lord Hardy
of Sheffield. Years ago he completed a small commission for
Madame Arnaud, who had recently taken particular interest
in the unfortunate Grace. He chose to deliver himself into
the hands of our forgiving and compassionate Lord this 8th
day of December.

—*Grenshire Argus* obituary, December 9, 1730

Wind seemed to swirl up and around the massive walls of the manor, as if we were trapped in a snow globe. My hair flew around my face, and I held it back with one hand. The air smelled of autumn, of cold air thieving leaves from their branches, of acorns settling down for a long period of secrecy inside the intimate kitchens of the squirrel.

The manor knew. And it wasn't happy.

"Too bad," I muttered.

With intention, I moved myself into the nursery, where I figured my family would be, wrapping up the evening, getting Tabby ready for bed. Miles and Eleanor followed; I felt the familiar tug from my chest and let them find me. We all of us, living and dead, gazed fondly at this sweet frowsy girl, currently being bundled into her ladybug pajamas.

I had never seen a more comforting sight.

Mom set her down on the floor while she went to get something.

I slathered Tabby in kisses. They weren't real, of course, just my face near her face.

But she reacted.

She turned away as if an overly eager dog had jumped on her. I looked over at Miles, who raised his eyebrows.

There was no reason now to get Tabby to tell Mom and Steven to leave the house, but I couldn't resist the chance to reach her. "It's Phoebe," I said in her ear. "Your sister, Phoebe. Remember me?"

"Phee sister," she said.

I whooped in excitement and turned to see if Mom had heard. She had. She came and sat on the floor next to us. She smiled sadly and, blinking with sudden tears, pulled Tabby into a hug. "I'm thinking of Phoebe, too," she said.

I looked over Mom's shoulder, and seeing Tabby's face I wanted to weep. She was as grief stricken as Mom, her face screwed into a rictus of sorrow. I'd thought she was too young to understand that I was gone . . . but she did.

I understood that for the rest of their lives, any moment of happiness, any surprised laugh, would always be followed with the reminder of me, the other member of the family, wrenched away in an instant. They'd always be etched with anguish, bold lines drawn forever on their souls.

Tabby and Mom hugged each other in a moment so wrought with agony that I wanted to shoot myself. I should've tried harder to explain to Mom about my fainting. I'd been defiant, sort of "screw you" about it, sort of "serves you right if I die"—but then I'd really died.

I was sixteen: I could've gone to the doctor alone if I'd taken responsibility for myself. I could've Googled *fainting*. Whatever. I could've tried harder.

My first job had been to save Tabby's life. Now that that was done, I wanted to figure out a way to tell Mom I was okay, that I didn't blame her.

I walked out of the nursery and nearly screamed at what I saw. Three maids stood in the hallway. One handed the other a stack of linens and the third was carrying a tray of tea. When they noticed me, they bobbed quick curtseys.

If I'd killed Madame Arnaud, why weren't these servants released?

I drifted around the hallways of the west wing, looking at those obscenely happy murals, the flocks of sheep that filed across the meadow to lay their soft heads in ladies' laps, the gentlemen crowning the duchesses with garlands of flowers they'd languidly woven themselves, as evidenced by the discarded blooms near their reclining legs. I wanted to make sure Madame Arnaud was gone, because the ghosts were still here. I was constantly sidestepping them: servants and children, as if nothing had happened.

I found my way to the room I'd been in before, then penetrated into the inner chamber, her bedroom. I creaked open the door and saw an enormous carved wooden box that took up nearly the entire room—a cupboard bed, meant to conserve heat in the days when no furnaces brought warm air through the night. I walked over and placed my hand on the paneling that I knew could be pulled open.

I slid open the panel. Dark tapestries covered the interior walls: hunters with their arrows still in the quiver but their faces aware of the prey before them, the deer who bent their tawny necks to survey the men behind them filing through the trees. A single candle rested on a shelf against the far wall, sending guttering light through the dimness and glinting off a brooch with the inscription of three x's. Shadows marched the walls like toy soldiers.

As my eyes adjusted, I saw feathers scattered everywhere; there were holes in the mattress.

"Nice try, Eleanor," I said, turning my head to address her. I'd felt from the tug in my chest that she had joined me.

"I spent many years here serving her," she said. "I haven't been back since the night I did this."

I held up a feather on my palm and blew it at her. "I think she's gone," I said. "But why are all the ghosts here?"

I thought about the toddler in the gardens. I especially wanted to deliver some peace to that poor tortured child. The servants didn't need to feel guilt any longer; they had done their time. And the children? Hopefully there were loving arms somewhere for them to be folded into.

"I don't know," said Eleanor. "I thought once Madame Arnaud was dead, everyone would be released."

"I thought so, too," I said.

I stared down at the snowy white feathers, mussed and erratic, as if a swan had gone through her death throes here. Whoever Madame Arnaud's lady's maid was, the one who replaced Eleanor, she hadn't bothered to repair or replace the mattress.

"Let's find Miles," I said. "We've got to figure something out."

We found him in the children's cemetery, staring moodily at a gravestone in front of him.

"There are still kids in the house," he said hoarsely.

"I know," I murmured. "What can we do?"

"I thought you did what we had to do," he said. "And I didn't expect to see this." He pointed to the gravestone.

LAVINIA WHITTLEBY
~
A Loss We Cannot Measure
A Cherub Called to the Stars
~
b. Feb. 16, 1799
d. Nov. 1, 1799

"That's my last name," he said.

I did the math, reluctantly. February to November—

Lavinia hadn't even been nine months old. She was one of the children, then, who didn't realize she was dead. He would never have seen her here at the manor, which was, I suppose, a good thing.

"Did your family ever speak of her?" Eleanor asked.

It took Miles a while to answer, and I saw he was shaking. "Never."

"I'm sorry," I whispered.

"Seventeen ninety-nine," he said. "How can I be sad about someone who died over two hundred years ago?"

"Very easily," I said. "Madame Arnaud is a monster. Of course you're upset about your ancestor."

I felt a twinge of guilt. I had nothing to do with this. I had fought a valiant fight; I had done everything I could. But looking at Miles's grim face, I realized that I was allied with the family that had caused this pain. I might even *be* an Arnaud, if his theory was right.

Miles was just one of hundreds who had cried throughout the generations, cried bitterly for the lost children and the empty cradles. They had tried to comfort each other around the firesides and tramped outside in the chill air to spit toward the manor hidden by its duplicitous greenery. So much hatred, so much helplessness.

"I'm sorry," I said again, but this time it was less about solace and more about feeling responsible to some degree.

He looked at me with an expression I can describe only as cold. His gaze swung back down again to his ancestor's stone. He seemed lost in some private reverie.

Eleanor gave me a significant look and walked away slowly, reading the names off other stones.

Below us, infant Lavinia tossed in her miniature pine box or whatever Madame Arnaud had deigned to pay for. Maybe nothing but dirt and leaves covered her. Maybe her burial had been nothing more than a hasty dig in the dirt by an aggrieved servant, who muttered the best prayers he could before Madame Arnaud summoned him back to more useful duties. Her parents had not had the chance to kneel here and say their good-byes . . . for all they knew, Madame Arnaud had tossed the small soul into the woods for the wolves to devour.

Lavinia's tiny fingers had never grown, never held anything of substance. Her skull remained a diminutive braincase. Odds are she'd never come to standing, merely lay helpless or crawled for the entirety of her short life. Although her mouth had issued cries and sounds, by nine months she'd never said a word, never been able to express to her family any semblance of the love she surely felt. She'd been deprived in the most profound way possible.

I stared at her stone and tried to broadcast my love down to her through the sod and worms, past the white, fibrous weed roots that dangled above her like stalactites.

I sent my love down through the beetles plodding past her bones or perching on them like they were skyscraper girders.

"Grow up, Lavinia," I said in my mind. "Come into your own."

Miles reached out a hand to touch her tombstone—
and the instant his fingers touched the surface, the world
changed.

That undercurrent of hushed voices, of sadness, that
Miles had taught me to listen to became a long, anticipa-
tory inrush of breath . . .

. . . then the deafening roar of a thousand voices
shouting. I clapped my hands to my ears, and fell to my
knees. The volume was so intense it felt like someone
was hitting every one of my teeth with a hammer. The
din washed through me and I could do nothing but open
my own mouth in a silent howl to relieve the pressure in
my ears.

The sound went on and on, scorching my brain, letting
no other stimuli enter my consciousness. It was like an
old locomotive train, oversized and made of iron, scraping along the rails, carving them into slices as it went.

Then, as if each of those shouting people realized how
fiendish they sounded, a respectful quiet fell. I let my
hands drop from my ears.

A bundle of light rose from Lavinia's grave and hung
in the air, golden and fragile as a prince's fairy-tale egg.

As I watched, awestruck, the light gently morphed and
stretched. It looked like a cocoon elongating as if a butterfly inside pushed. I squinted my eyes . . . what was
blurry and light-dazzling became more clear. Hanging in
midair was a baby slumbering under a blanket.

The blanket rolled back as if by a mother's loving fingers, and the infant's limbs stretched and fattened.

The fingers lengthened . . . the spine stretched.

I looked deep into the throb of light and found the child's eyes. She was staring at Miles with a gentle admiration. But the babyish expression soon altered; she grew some understanding. Her eyes sharpened.

She was twice the size now, growing and translucent. I could see her name on the tombstone through her shining body. She slid through toddlerhood and into girlhood. She lost her pudgy cheeks. I grabbed Miles's hand.

She continued growing older. Her face changed significantly, and lean legs surged down out of her body. Her clothing changed—no longer the short pinafore of a child, but the long skirts of a young woman. Her arms and legs became muscular.

The scant curls that the eight-month-old had first shown us had grown from her head continuously the whole time, like a mechanical loom spitting out weave. The now thick, luxuriant hair pulled itself back tightly into a proper bun. Her feet nearly touched the ground, but she still hovered an inch or so above. She was our height, slightly older than Miles and me. She glimmered there, solid and sure of herself.

A cap appeared on her head, and her dress instantly went black. She spread her arms and a bibbed apron tucked itself through them. "She would have been a maid if she lived," whispered Miles.

"We've been waiting so long," said Lavinia in a voice like an old record, slightly warped. "We despaired that our families would ever come for us."

Out of the corner of my eye, I saw golden light emerge from another grave. And another. Now, lights were everywhere, like a klatch of fireflies. Each grave was offering up its inhabitant. The shine of these children fought away the darkness.

They all started at different ages—whenever they'd been killed, I guessed. It was like those time-lapse movies they showed us in grade school, where a seedling pokes from the soil, wavers toward the sky, thickens and produces a bud, then a bloom, all in ten seconds.

The children cycled quickly through their would-be lives, from infant to toddler to child to teen with breathtaking speed, to land on what looked like their early twenties. Why? Why were they all roughly the same age?

I surveyed the shining adults suspended over their graves, regarding us with serious faces. I kept watching until it dawned on me. They were all at their most vital stage, men with muscled forearms, women ready to step onto the ground with quick step. A few were quite old, which made me realize strength didn't always have to do with age.

"You can release them," I said. "Miles, you're the only one here connected to the children—to one of them."

Eleanor had crept back to us, and seized my hand. I stared up at the glowing people and an idea inserted itself into my mind. I had been able to vanquish Madame Arnaud because I was an Arnaud. I swallowed as I admitted this to myself.

Miles could release the children because he was related to one of them. Lavinia had even said they'd been waiting for their families to come.

Miles took a step backward until he could hold my other hand. We stood together, the three of us, firm and strong.

"I release you," he said. "I'm sorry your families couldn't come for you. I'm here now. And I'm so sorry."

I closed my eyes in relief, thinking these were the words that mattered. The children would be gone when I opened them.

And perhaps Eleanor could release the servants, because she had been a servant in this house. We were a mighty triumvirate. We each had a role to play, a specific part that required us to be united with one another. It had something to do with the good force around the house. It had sent me to Eleanor's room to find her diary, but Madame Arnaud had interfered. It was the second time—with Miles—that we'd found our ally through her diary.

Maybe once we'd each done our particular job, we would release ourselves.

I would be so sad to say good-bye to Miles—and now to Eleanor, too. I would want one last glance at my mom, at Tabby . . . and at the man who was perhaps . . . no, who undoubtedly *was* my father.

I opened my eyes. The children were still there. I looked at Miles's face in profile. I saw a muscle in his jaw twitch: he was grinding his teeth. Frustrated.

I heard Eleanor gasp and whipped my head around. Coming through the gates of the cemetery was a long parade of the servants. They came, hundreds of them, and formed in regimented lines facing the children. It reminded me of how servants would come outside the manor to greet important guests, arranging themselves in their obvious servitude.

They were sobbing.

Even the men, stoic, had tears running down their cheeks.

"We need someone to speak for us," said Maud Pike, the maid who had been looking for Cook for her orders. She pointed to Eleanor. "You're the one to do it."

Eleanor bowed her head and I thought she was going to refuse. When she lifted her head, her face was streaked with tears.

"I will," she said. "I will humbly and with great remorse speak for the servants." I squeezed her hand and she squeezed back.

She pivoted her head around, giving eye contact to each of the grown children in turn, a long, silent passage of acknowledgment, flowing to and from them.

"Children came into this household," she said. "And better than the somber issue of the Arnauds, you village children knew how to laugh. That is, if you were old enough to. The high spirits you brought to the manor . . . well, at first we thought 'twas a fine and good thing. Who can ever hear a child chortling down a hallway and not get up to grinning oneself?

"It took us a bit to understand what was truly going on. Rumblings among the servants who saw the feeding chamber firsthand. But it is difficult, almost impossible, to believe in such a vile and desperate bit of gossip."

The children watched her quietly.

"By the time we fully grasped what was happening, we felt it was too late. Children were already dead. We didn't know what to do. We would pass the word along to the new servants, thinking they might have the energy to do what we were too foolish to try . . . and so time passed. Children, I eventually got up my courage. I tried to kill Madame Arnaud—but I failed."

She ran her hands over her cap in a gesture of complete and utter disconsolation. "I failed at the only important thing I could have ever done."

"You tried," cried slender Maud Pike, her face twisted in concern. "You tried and the saints bless ye for it!"

"And 'twas your death that let me leave this hell-forsaken place," said another servant, a man I hadn't seen before. "After the day the village uprose, I returned to a simple honest life, as did most of us that had been in service here."

Eleanor turned to me and gave me a shocked look. How had her death helped?

"What wretchedness has plagued the stones of this manor," said Lavinia, before I could follow the line of reasoning. "It is a doomed place of much sadness."

She was as transparent as convent-made crystal, seemingly frail, but her voice carried. "I forgive you, all of you," she said.

The servants of one accord gave a raw moan.

"Bless you, dear girl," said Eleanor.

"You're my family," said Miles to Lavinia. "I hope you find peace now."

Lavinia gave him a rueful smile, then disappeared. Not in the vapory slow way I would expect; she vanished as if someone had snapped his fingers.

Another man cleared his throat. He was a plowman and held a bread-sized stone dislodged centuries ago. Its pitted surface still held soil from the Arnaud fields. "I forgive you, all of you," he said. He gave a brief nod, as if for a job neatly completed, and disappeared.

A laundress spoke up, holding her basket of washing to her tilted hip. "I forgive you, all of you," she said. She winked out like a lamp.

A seamstress, a chambermaid with her ash-filled bucket and brush, a blacksmith with his anvil lightly floating by his feet, a stablehand holding leather, a scullery maid with her sleeves rolled up to her elbows, on and on. Each one took their turn with dignity.

I saw the toddler from the back gardens; he had lost his feral look as he became an affable-looking gentleman who held a black medical bag.

Miles and I shared a look. "Thank God," he said.

When the last glowing being had extinguished, I turned to look at the rank of servants. I could barely see them in the dark. I was aware of their shapes, grieving and yet exhilarated. One woman untied her apron and threw it to the side. It landed on one of the tombstones. It looked like one of the monuments in the family's graveyard, where a sculpted mantle draped an urn.

"Our work here is finally done," said Eleanor to the gathered servants.

Ice filled my gut as I watched all of them turn their

gaze to me. Eleanor, too. She let go of my hand and went to stand with them.

I understood this at the deepest level possible. They saw me as the mistress of the house.

"I . . ." I faltered. Miles stepped closer to me so I could lean against his shoulder.

"I release you all. I thank you for your years of good and faithful service." I closed my eyes, moved beyond belief—and sickened to think I truly was an Arnaud.

When I opened them, the servants were gone. Without a word, as they'd done all their lives, they'd withdrawn silently. Only Eleanor remained, looking frightened.

But . . . what about us? We'd conquered Madame Arnaud, we'd released the children, freed the servants . . . wasn't that the mission we had to accomplish, to be able to move on to whatever stage death held for us?

"I don't get it," said Miles.

"Why didn't I go with them?" cried Eleanor. I let go of Miles's hand and rushed to her, enfolding her in a fierce embrace.

"Looks like we're all still stuck together," I said.

Miles gave me a determined, cockeyed grin, but Eleanor could not be consoled. He and I had been dead only awhile. She'd spent over a century in that state, and she wanted release.

"Eleanor, we'll figure it out," I pleaded with her. "There's another step we're missing. There's something else we have to do."

"What else could there be?" she implored. "The house is punishing me for trying to kill Madame Arnaud."

"But you told us there had been other attempts on her life," said Miles. "You're the only servant left standing."

"I wish Austin was here," she said, wiping away a tear. I nodded. Death wasn't so lonely for me . . . my family was alive, and I had Miles. She didn't have anyone.

"You did a wonderful thing," Miles said, lifting her chin. "You were a leader for the servants, and you knew exactly what to say to the children."

Sometimes it seemed like Eleanor might be a better choice for Miles than I was. I felt like I should turn my head away from such intimacy.

"You did," I said. "You were perfect."

"Thank you," she said, blushing. It was so strange to see just a trace of tint on her wan face. We still experienced living emotions, but they were incredibly muted.

"You were perfect, too, miss," she said. "I can't even imagine how you went underwater like that, with her down there with you."

"How can you call me 'miss' after all this?" I asked. "You are absolutely my equal. I don't know if I could have stabbed her while she slept."

We looked at each other warmly, shyly.

"You would have," she said quietly. She leaned over and pressed a kiss to my cheek. My sister of sorts. This was the kiss Tabby would never be able to give me.

"Miles didn't perform too shabbily, either," I remarked, and laughed . He pretended to be offended for my benefit, staring stonily into the distance.

"No, he was a true champion," said Eleanor with admiration clear in her voice.

Oh dear. I wondered if Miles and I would ever get close again. I flashed to our night kissing in his bed, and quickly suppressed the memory.

"Let's go see my sister," I said huskily. I felt Miles put his hands on my shoulders from behind. I felt as good as it was possible to feel.

Everyone was asleep. Mom and Steven lay in bed in the master bedroom, which I peeked into as we progressed down the hall. Good for them, I thought, asleep to everything, buffered from trouble. They had no idea of the spectacle that had taken place. They had no idea I was with them, stuck on some plateau between life and death. For them was still reserved the pleasure, the absolute climactic swooning contentment, of being able to sleep.

Down the hall, and in the pool of light cast by the night-light, Tabby slumbered, too.

CHAPTER SEVENTEEN

Even a cursory perusal of the microfilm shows how despondent was the life of servants in the earlier part of the nineteenth century. An abundance of suicide was reported in the pages of the *Grenshire Argus,* a paper first publishing in January of 1715 in the small, rural town of Grenshire. A large manor house built there in 1721 employed hundreds of servants over the years, and a strikingly disproportionate number of these took their own lives. Rather than assume cruel behavior on the part of the masters there, this paper shall examine "life in service" in general, and the socioeconomic and psychological reasons behind this rash of suicide.

—From Trudy Bilkington's sociology senior thesis,
University of York, 2008

*G*ood things.

Good things were happening.

It turned out some of the books in the Arnaud library were rare editions, and Steven was planning to sell them to antique book collectors. They would bring in an astounding amount of money—Madame Arnaud had in particular spirited out one of Louis XIV's diaries, and the discovery was going to cause an international sensation. A few years ago, a fake diary had been published, and Steven had an appointment with scholars and conservators to verify this book's authenticity.

Something else arose out of the pending book sales. Interest in the manor.

The town's residents had so carefully hushed up the

story of Madame Arnaud that the grandiosity of her estate was also lost to the outside world. The National Trust, a group that preserves important homes, was beside itself with the chance to have a basically untouched manor from the early 1700s, with a link to the French royal court, to adopt as a project. So maybe those lawns would again be bright green and the gardens full of flowers.

Miles, Eleanor, and I took regular tours of the manor to be sure Madame Arnaud was gone, and that no left-behind ghosts lingered. "What do you think will happen when your mom and dad find the children's cemetery?" asked Miles. We were standing in the same spot where, earlier, we'd first discovered that lost, angry boy. I was tempted to correct his use of the word *dad,* but wondered if it really was the correct term.

Standing just below Miles on the rise, I looked at his solidness against the backdrop of the manor. He looked like the master of the property. He was magisterial, far older than his years somehow. I pictured him in jodhpurs and a long velvet coat, holding a riding crop: England itself.

"I have no idea," I answered honestly. Would they understand what they saw? Who would give them the village gossip about Madame Arnaud, as Miles had done for me? And would it be delivered with a wink and a grin . . . or with a believer's solemnity?

"The unfortunate thing is, the human hunger for scandal and bloodthirst probably means the National Trust can capitalize on the cemetery," said Miles. "They'll probably charge extra to access that portion of the grounds."

I thought how horrible it was that some gleeful sense of the macabre might spur people to visit the children's cemetery, without any understanding that real people had been hurt. I remembered when, as a child, I'd begged Mom to let me visit the torture chamber area of the Ripley's Believe It or Not! museum at the San Francisco waterfront . . . and how I'd burst into tears when I realized that those instruments had actually been used on people.

"Maybe they'll have a sense of propriety about it," I said. "Maybe they'll lock it up and keep people out."

"Isn't it wild to think tour buses will roll up, and people will be picnicking here?" Miles asked. "The Versailles of Britain, that's how they'll market it."

"I for one think it shall be pleasant to have happy people here on holiday," said Eleanor. "It's too big an estate for just one family without servants."

I smiled. It was true; the servants were part of what made the house feel full—or at least I imagined that was the case in the manor's heyday.

"And as for us? Will we be happy?" asked Miles.

I couldn't answer that question and avoided his eyes. "We need to learn more about the history here," I said. "I wish we had your Austin. It seems like there are conflicting pagan forces, and we need to destroy one and enable the other."

"I used to do that all the time when I was alive," said Miles nonchalantly. I burst out laughing.

"I shall be happy," said Eleanor stoutly. "I've spent years upon years in my narrow room, guilt filled and lonelier than you can probably imagine. Now I have two wonderful companions to fill my days with pleasant conversation."

"There could be worse places to be stuck," I admitted.

I wanted to learn more about the runes I'd seen on the tree in the woodland pool, and figure out how we were all to "graduate." But I had to shrug. It was nothing I could control. And it would be nice to keep an eye on Tabby, watch her grow into an adult . . . just like that maid had said she'd done with her favorite brother . . . and to see my mom and Steven heal from my death.

Which reminded me.

I reclined on the living room carpet next to Tabby, running my fingers through the shag, feeling it massage under my fingernails. How sad that the house offered tactility when I craved the human touch instead: the soft fat-filled cheek of Tabby, my mom's perfumed neck.

I'd been working on Tabby for a few days now. She reacted to me only in a very minor way, and unpredictably. Sometimes it seemed she heard me as plainly as if I were still alive; other times, I'd chant until my tongue tired and she heard nothing.

I'd tried various phrases. I'd worked on the word *forgive*—just in case Mom really thought I blamed her for not listening to me about the fainting—but for some reason Tabby often refused to say it.

I'd tried "Phoebe loves you" and "Phoebe misses you"

and all the various permutations of that concept. Tabby was able to get some of them out, but never in the way I'd fantasized about, with Mom and Steven sitting, rapt and attentive, waiting for her next words.

I once got Tabby to say "Phee forgive" and I'd shouted with excitement, but Mom had turned on the garbage disposal at that very minute and no one heard. I dogged Tabby for an hour after that, but she wouldn't repeat it.

Today I was giving it a rest, just enjoying watching her place animal shapes into a puzzle. They were the wooden kind with pegs attached to the back, so they could be lowered into their carved-out silhouettes. Sometimes she tried to put them in upside down. I marveled that her brain wasn't yet ready to notice that. It was so very obvious! But I had to give her credit for noticing something that no one else in the house could: me.

Steven was lounging on the floor next to her, lightly helping. His reclined body and mine formed an acute angle, with Tabby in the middle as our bisector. Across the room, Mom was sitting on the sofa knitting. She'd never done that in California—probably a hobby taken up to keep her mind busy, to keep her from thinking about me. It looked like she was making a hat for Tabby, with a deep eggplant-colored yarn. The winter here in Grenshire would be cold.

My mind went back to my own childhood, to the handmade things Mom had created for me. She didn't knit but she did sew, and for my eighth birthday she'd given me the most beautiful doll. *Eglantine*.

Eglantine had a muslin face on which Mom had carefully applied oil paints, to make remarkably realistic features. Her eyes were the same green as mine. Even though I didn't know why at the time, I remembered Mom mixing up the paint, holding the plastic pallet right up to my eyes, adding in more white, more viridian, squeezing her tubes until she got a color that matched. Somehow she even painted a nice blush on the doll's cheeks, without it looking blatant.

Eglantine's hair was flax. Mom had sent away for it on the internet, sewed it onto her head, and plaited it in a loose, Germanic braid. Eglantine had a red goose-girl kerchief that was removable.

The clothes were what were so stunning. Making her own patterns, Mom had sewn a little alpine dirndl. The close-fitting burgundy corset had miniature silver buttons that truly worked, through quarter-inch buttonholes. Her loden skirt had a jacquard ribbon trim along the bottom, with a white eyelet apron over it. Eglantine wasn't a particularly German name, but it's what I assigned her.

She was my constant companion for two weeks, sitting on my lap in the car, propped up on the bathroom counter to watch me brush my teeth, tucked into bed beside me. Then I lost her.

To this day, I had no idea where she went. It wasn't the sort of situation where you have a toy before you go somewhere and don't have it afterward, so you know you lost it there, whether or not you can retrieve it.

No. Somehow although all my waking thoughts had been of Eglantine, I couldn't nail down when I'd lost track of her.

Mom had been furious. So much labor had gone into the doll, and I'd been careless of something I clearly loved. I'd begged her to make me another, but she claimed it wasn't possible. I think she wanted to teach me a lesson about guarding valuable things. Ironic.

Now, as I watched her fingers swiftly moving in strange controlled gestures with the knitting needles dully clicking, it occurred to me that someone from another culture might wonder what ritualistic behavior she indulged in, what spells she cast. All the while the purple swath of weave grew magically, row by row.

I wished I could shout out Eglantine's name, make Mom's face bloom in memory of the doll who'd been lost nearly a decade ago.

Ohhhhhhhh.

I *could,* in a manner of speaking.

Holy sweet Jesus. If I could coach Tabby to say *Eglantine,* there was no doubt Mom would know I was in some way still with them. First of all: three syllables. Not something Tabby would come up with on her own. Secondly: an oddball name. I'd never before or since met another Eglantine. They say monkeys could type randomly for hundreds of years and come up with a Shakespearean play . . . but I didn't think Tabby could ever put together those particular syllables on her own.

I was energized by the idea. Eglantine would be the key to open the door of their attention. Once Tabby said that, they'd *listen.*

I lay for a while, just enjoying the sensation of anticipation. It's not an emotion very often experienced by the dead. Perhaps called to me by that rawness of sensation, Miles and Eleanor were suddenly there.

"What's up?" asked Miles.

"I have an idea to get through to Mom and Steven," I said. I ran through the story quickly. Their faces registered the same warm excitement I felt. Eleanor took a seat next to Mom on the sofa to watch, while Miles became another spoke to our wheel, lying on his stomach, propping his chin up on his palms. Seen from above, we would appear like a child's drawing of a four-petaled daisy.

I leaned over and kissed Tabby's hand as it struggled to place a horse in its painted pasture. Of course, I was kissing only where I believed the hand to be, because no skin was there to meet my lips—or rather, no lips to meet her skin. She dropped the puzzle piece.

I grinned.

"Oops, here you go," said Steven, handing it back to her.

She carefully lowered it, correctly oriented, head to head, and tail to tail with the depression carved out to receive it; and I kissed her hand again. "Phee!" she protested as she again dropped it.

Miles whooped. "She knows it's you!" he exulted.

Predictably, Steven didn't seem to react to her shortening of my name. I guess she hadn't really been talking much before I died, not enough for him to recognize her version of *Phoebe*.

I savored the moment. I was beginning a process that

would change everything. And as frustrating as it was to not have Mom and Steven know I was there, it was frightening to think of how astounded—and possibly disturbed—they'd be when they learned.

And . . . it would never permit them to let go of me, either, I realized. I wanted the family to heal. I didn't want to be forgotten, necessarily, but I wanted them to be able to go forward and take pleasure from life.

Should I really do this? Wouldn't Mom and Steven be better off *not* knowing their dead teen watched their every movement?

"I didn't really think this through," I said. I sat up abruptly. Miles crawled over to me—*through* Tabby, I noticed with a flinch—and took my hand.

"What's going on?" he asked.

"I know this will work," I said. "And I'm not sure I want it to."

"Why?"

"I want Mom and Steven to go on to build their life. They moved all the way across the world to get away from the idea of me—and now I'm going to blow their minds by telling them I came along, too?"

"But didn't you want to tell your mom you didn't blame her? About not listening to you when you were worried about fainting?" The pressure from his hand was comforting; he continued to squeeze long past the time most people would simply revert to holding.

"Yes, but . . ."

I struggled to put into words what I felt.

"You want to deliver that message and then essentially disappear," said Eleanor from the sofa.

"Exactly!" I said.

"Well . . . you can do that," said Eleanor.

I thought for a while until I figured out what they meant. I could get Mom to understand I forgave her, then I could say good-bye. She didn't need to know that I didn't really leave. I'd be the person who pretends to end a phone call but stays on the line.

"I see what you're saying," I said.

"It's a good idea," said Miles.

"Thanks, Eleanor," I said, smiling across the room at her. I prepared. Poor Mom, knitting away furiously to create something bright to adorn her daughter's head, and Steven, placidly helping place puzzle pieces with Zen-like patience . . . their world would never be the same again.

Their questions about death, the afterlife, would be answered by knowing their dead child could communicate with them.

There would be tears, I knew. There would be an out-gush of emotion so unedited that it would splinter the souls of each of us here. It would wring me out, exhaust me, make me experience anew the catastrophe of having died.

But I needed to do it. I couldn't stand the idea that Mom constantly replayed in her mind the discussion that day, when I'd told her I'd fainted and she'd laughed and told me to keep breathing when talking to cute guys.

I let go of Miles's hand and leaned in closer to Tabby. She did something she'd never done before. She raised her gaze and looked at me.

I felt it deep to my core, a stabbing impact to my very heart, or what was left of it.

"Oh, Tabby," I whispered.

She continued to level her gaze at me, with those eyes that appeared huge since the face enclosing them was so small. Everything about her was perfect, untouched, curved with the beautiful lines of childhood.

"Phee," she said.

"Oh thank God, Tabby," I said, tears welling up in my eyes. "You see me."

"Here you go," said Steven. He was trying to hand her a puzzle piece. "What are you staring at?" He waved his hands in front of her face. "Earth to Tabby!"

Mom laughed. "Her teen spaciness begins already. It's a little early, Tabby!"

Tabby and I looked at each other for long moments, serious and intense as lovers. *She sees me.*

"Tabby, I need you to say a word for me," I said, my voice trembling through the tears.

She waited.

"The word is Eglantine. Can you please say it?"

She just looked at me, sadness pouring all over her features. It was so *wrong*. No one that young should have that adult expression of wretchedness. A toddler's rounded face should show nothing but glee and wonder at the new things the world showed them on a daily basis.

"Eglantine," I repeated. "Can you say it for me?"

"Phee," she said.

I buried my face in my hands. This was too much for me. She *missed* me. She longed for me, her older sister who had barely paid her any attention when alive. I hadn't realized how much a part of her small world I was.

"I miss you, Tabby," I said. "I love you so much, and I wish I could be there for you. I'm so sorry I left."

She nodded.

"Tabby?" asked Steven.

"Miss you," she said.

My hands uselessly stroked in the air for her. I wanted to hug her, to fix the crazy cowlick of her hair and tuck the wayward strand behind her ears. I wanted to hold her pudgy hands and swing her around and around the room. I'd done that, I remembered. I'd swung her. I'd given her something, a few episodes of hysterical laughter as I made her, like me, completely dizzy.

"I miss you *so* much," I said.

She burst into tears. The howls of unselfconscious agony only young children are capable of.

"What *is* it?" asked Steven. He and Mom were on her now, hugging and trying to soothe. "She just started spacing out, and then this," he told Mom.

"Eglantine," I said. "Say it, Tabby."

She couldn't say anything; she was hyperventilating. "Take some breaths," said Mom at the exact same time I said it.

That was a gift. Tabby laughed at the surprise of this synchronicity, and instantly her tears were gone. The thundercloud of the toddler: so quickly storming, so quickly sailing off to someone else's sky.

"Eglantine," I said, although it broke my heart to insist. This was the moment. Everything was going to change. Right now.

"Eggwantine," said Tabby.

Mom drew back from Tabby as if she were a fire that had burned her. "*What* did you say?" she said, her face an intense, focused machine.

"Oh, Mom," I said softly.

"Eggwantine," said Tabby.

Mom looked wildly to Steven. "That doll!" she said, her voice a gurgle of barely controlled hysteria. "Phoebe's doll. Tabitha wasn't even born yet!"

"What are you talking about?" said Steven.

"I made a . . . doll . . . when she was eight, when . . . Don and I were still—" She could barely get it out, her breath hitching and gasping. She was out of air just as if she had fallen from a tree and had the breath knocked out of her.

That's right. Mom was married to my dad back then. Even Steven didn't know about the doll. Eglantine was the perfect code word for just me and Mom to share.

"So why is Tabby . . . ?" asked Steven.

"Oh my God, my God, my God, my God, my God," said Mom. "Tabby, what do you know? What do you know?" She grabbed Tabby's shoulders so hard that Tabby gave a little cry.

Tabby extracted her left arm enough to point to me. "Phee here," she said.

Mom screamed.

"What the hell?" shouted Steven. "What the hell is going on?"

"It's okay, Phoebe, it's okay," said Miles to me. "Just let it happen. They'll be okay."

"Tell them I love them," I said to Tabby. I couldn't stop crying, but I managed to keep my breath so I could talk. It would be too frustrating to come this far and not be able to communicate. I focused as hard as I could on quelling the emotions that threatened to shred me to nothing.

But Tabby couldn't say it. We were still intermittent, like a radio station tuning in and out.

"Phoebe is *here*?" Mom asked, when she could speak again. She scanned where Tabby had pointed, but her eyes glossed over me as if I weren't there.

"Eggwantine," she said again. Oh, poor Tabby, she was on stage and no one had handed her a script.

"Tell them I love them," I said again. I positioned my face right in front of hers, and it worked: she nodded.

"Phee love you," she announced.

Mom dug her fingernails deep into her own cheeks. When she removed them a moment later, to instead dig them into Steven's arm, eight little perfect half-moons of blood marked her face.

"Phoebe!" Mom screamed. "Phoebe!" Her screaming softened to a wail. "I can't see you!"

"I forgive you," I said. This time I said it to her directly. Tabby didn't pick it up and repeat it. "I forgive you, Mom."

"This is crazy," said Steven. "Anne, she isn't here. There's no possible way she's here."

"But she *said,*" said Mom. "She said—Eglantine."

"She must've heard about the doll before Phoebe died," he said.

"No!" shouted Mom. "That doll was lost eight years ago. This is real, Steven. Phoebe's here, she's here . . . Oh, my sweetheart, I miss you so much." Her eyes, with large dilated pupils, looked around the room wildly, as if trying to track a fly too fast to catch a glimpse of.

"I forgive you, Mom," I said again. I felt Miles's hand steal back into mine. I glanced over at Eleanor, still sitting on the sofa, watching with compassionate eyes. "Can you tell her, Tabby?" I prompted.

"Phee say forgive," said Tabby finally. She crawled into Mom's lap, throwing her arms around her neck. Mom broke down, sobbing into Tabby's hair.

"I can't see you, I can't see you," she kept saying.

"It's okay," I said.

"It's okay," Tabby repeated.

"I forgive you," I coached.

"Forgive," said Tabby.

Mom rocked back and forth with Tabby, sobbing. Steven sat there with his mouth open, shaking his head over and over. "This isn't happening," he said in a voice so low I wouldn't have caught it if I hadn't happened to be looking at him right then.

A long time later, Mom lifted her head again. Her face was as blotchy as a map rendered only in shades and tones of red. Her eyes were so bloodshot they made her green irises a weird and intense stained-glass rose window.

"You forgive me?" she asked the air plaintively. She had heard, then.

"Yes," I said simply.

"I'm so sorry, Phoebe," she said. "I should have listened to you. I've wanted to kill myself a hundred times over that I didn't listen. I've wished I were . . . like you." She couldn't say the word *dead*, I saw.

"It's not your fault," I said. "Tabby, tell her. Not your fault."

"Nawfawt," said Tabby.

"Not your fault," I corrected.

"Naw y'fawt."

Mom got it. "How can you say it's not my fault?" she said despairingly. "They said if you'd been diagnosed, there were medications—" She broke into a fresh batch of crying.

There was so much I wanted to express, too much to be able to fit through the small funnel of Tabby's mouth. I felt blame, too; after all, I had been nearly an adult and could've made a better argument for seeking medical care.

I also wanted to tell her about Madame Arnaud, how proud I was that I'd been the one to figure out how to kill her, and that I'd entered the water again to accomplish it. That I'd saved Tabby from a terrible death. There was simply no way to express all that: and maybe it was best for her not to know how close Tabby had come to being Madame Arnaud's next victim.

I just needed to let Mom know I was at rest, although I wasn't.

And say good-bye forever.

"My fault, too," I said, simplifying my language so it would be easy for Tabby to parrot back.

Tabby looked at me with her eyes full and moist. "Phee's fawt," she said.

Mom moaned, her voice rising in pitch until it was soprano. "It was never, never, never your fault," she said fiercely. "I am your mom. It was my job to protect you."

Steven joined the conversation, pulling himself out of the head-shaking repetition he'd put himself into. "Anne, don't fight it. Phoebe's trying to tell you it's okay. She doesn't blame you, doesn't blame us."

Mom looked at him, and he pulled her and Tabby together into a passionate hug.

"She's come back to tell us it's all right," he said. "We need to do her the favor of listening."

Listening, yes, I rejoiced! All I ever wanted: for them to listen!

Mom nodded while he used his shirt hem to dry her face. "Okay," she said in a shaky voice. "You're right."

"Phoebe, we love you and miss you *so much,*" said Steven. He didn't bother to try to guess where I might be; he said the words tenderly to Mom as if she were my proxy. "We wish we had done everything differently, but thank you for telling us you forgive us."

God bless you, Steven! I thought. I looked into his face for signs that he was my real dad. I had to conclude that even if he wasn't my biological father, he was still truly, truly my father.

And now it was time for me to draw the curtain closed. Mom and Steven already had enough to absorb; I couldn't add more to their list of reality-shaking concepts to contemplate.

"I have to go," I said. Eleanor nodded sadly but encouragingly at me.

"No!" said Tabby.

"I'm so sorry," I said to her. "You're the best little sister I could have ever hoped for. I have to go now, though."

I longed to tell her I'd keep an eye out for her, and be there to cheer her on as she grew, but I didn't want to confuse my good-bye. The thought struck me, though, that if she continued to hone her skills at detecting me, she might know I was there anyway.

Who knows what the future holds, I thought. *I can't control it. All I can do is try to make it so my family hurts the least amount possible.*

"Good-bye, sweetheart," I said.

"No! Phee stay!" she said in her voice that threatened of a coming tantrum.

"Oh no, no, Tabby," I said warningly. I almost cracked a smile at the idea I was scolding her from the other side. "Be a good girl. Don't get upset. I have to go. Say good-bye to mom and your dad for me."

It didn't work. She started to make the huffy chorts of a fit. Damn! This was hardly the elegant, poignant way I wanted to withdraw from my family forever.

"Tabby! Sh!" I said.

Miles looked at me and started laughing.

"Is Phoebe leaving?" Mom asked her. "Phoebe, no, stay!" She looked as stricken as she had the day the coroner told her my disease had been preventable.

This was all falling apart.

"Let her go," said Steven, the voice of reason. "You want her to go to a place of peace, don't you? Don't force her to stay."

Great thinking, Steven. Except that there is no peace for me. Not yet. Not that I know of.

"Noooo," wailed Tabby. She crawled out of Mom's lap. Her hands formed into fists and she beat them against her puzzle board on the floor. The pieces that had already been placed—unwitting chickens and piglets who had been minding their own business—sprang into the air.

Argh! Why did she have to ruin such a touching moment?

But then I swallowed. She wasn't upset because she wasn't getting her way. She was upset because she thought she'd never see me again. And that realization was enough to send me somewhere else momentarily.

The blue water, the Grenshire pool, the lanes defined by bobbing buoys, shouts of kids echoing off the high ceiling . . .

No.

I pulled myself back. I had to see this through.

Why was I lying to Tabby? I wasn't saying good-bye forever. How hard would it be for me to tell her—and only her—the truth? She could handle it better than Mom and Steven.

I came back to the living room to the pure, loud melee of Tabby's tantrum, and Mom and Steven's bewildered, confused attempts to control it.

"Okay, Tabby, here's what's going to happen," I said, squatting down next to her. "You can sense me. They can't. I'll keep coming to see you . . . but Mom and Steven can't know."

She stopped sobbing abruptly.

"It hurts them too much to know I'm here," I said. "I'll explain it better when you're older. But you'll still sense me, Tabby. I'll still be here."

"Okay," she said. She ran her fist under her nose to wipe away the gunk.

"What's okay?" asked Mom. "Tell us what she said."

"Phee go bye," said Tabby.

My eyes narrowed. Toddlers tell lies! They do!

I walked around the room, bending to give kisses to each of them. Only Tabby raised her head for hers.

"All right," I said. "We should go."

"Good-bye, my sweet, my love, my girl. My firstborn," said Mom.

"Good-bye, my mom, my love, the person I love best in the whole world," I said. She didn't hear me, but on her face I saw the smallest indication of a smile. She'd known that in the pause after she spoke, I would have said some loving words in return.

"Good-bye, dear Phoebe," said Steven. "I love you as if you were my own daughter."

"You, too, Steven. And in every way that matters, you *are* my dad," I said.

"Bye," said Tabby offhandedly when it was her turn. She was already okay with the idea, knowing I'd be back.

"You're special," I told her. "I protected you from Madame Arnaud, and I'll protect you as best I can in the years to come."

Eleanor and Miles came to me. "You did very well," Eleanor said to me.

"You did *great*," said Miles.

With our arms intertangled in one another's, in a triad of a hug, we left. For now.

We left as my mom's skin burned from all her hot tears, and she took ragged breaths to calm herself down, alternating between fresh tears and huge, tremulous smiles of incredulity. We left as Steven replayed the entire disjointed conversation in his mind, dissecting it like a scientist. There'd be many, many discussions in the future, with he and Mom polishing the words that traveled from my mouth to Tabby's, remembering them, savoring them. Figuring them out. My last glance, however, was for Tabby, sitting back down to her puzzle with all the nonchalance of infancy.

ACKNOWLEDGMENTS

Thanks for a wide variety of reasons to Alan Howard, Jenny Phillips, Nikisha Vashee, Abby Heiser, Joe Quirk, Ki Longfellow, Traci Foust, Jessy and Deborah Krant and Tamim Ansary, Cinda Meister and Brad Jones, Kelly Young, Marly Rusoff and Michael Radulescu, Julie Mosow, Ariana Rosado-Fernández, James Davie, Kathryn L. Rizqallah, Susan Spann, Jenny D. Williams, Alison McMahan, and Michelle Gagnon. Sometimes you are lucky enough to make a writing friend who will read your novel not just once or twice, but *three* times: huge thanks to Jordan Rosenfeld. Finally, thanks to Michaela Hamilton, Randie Lipkin, and the wonderful team at Kensington.

Don't miss the next novel in the Arnaud Legacy series
by Lynn Carthage

BETRAYED

Coming from Kensington in 2016!